"I need your help." Dead

Uh-oh. "My help?"

"OK, let me start from the beginning." He pauses for a moment. "I'm Deadpool. You may have heard of me. I'm kind of a big deal. Fifth spot on the Ranker list of greatest super heroes last time I checked. Would you believe Spider-Man is on the top spot? It's really depressing. What's he got that I haven't – apart from being sticky? Anyhow. It's me. Surprise! I'm on a really important secret mission, given to me by Daredevil. Or was that part secret too? I've got a bad feeling that there is a lot more to it than I know, though. Isn't there always? So I'm worried about everything going wrong. Did I mention that I used to be an Avenger?"

The day is turning really strange, and it's only going to get worse...

ALSO AVAILABLE

MULTIVERSE MISSIONS
She-Hulk Goes to Murderworld by Tim Dedopulos

MARVEL CRISIS PROTOCOL
Target: Kree by Stuart Moore
Shadow Avengers by Carrie Harris

MARVEL HEROINES
Domino: Strays by Tristan Palmgren
Rogue: Untouched by Alisa Kwitney
Elsa Bloodstone: Bequest by Cath Lauria
Outlaw: Relentless by Tristan Palmgren
Black Cat: Discord by Cath Lauria

LEGENDS OF ASGARD
The Head of Mimir by Richard Lee Byers
The Sword of Surtur by C L Werner
The Serpent and the Dead by Anna Stephens
The Rebels of Vanaheim by Richard Lee Byers
Three Swords by C L Werner

SCHOOL OF X
The Siege of X-41 by Tristan Palmgren

MARVEL UNTOLD
The Harrowing of Doom by David Annandale
Dark Avengers: The Patriot List by David Guymer
Witches Unleashed by Carrie Harris
Reign of the Devourer by David Annandale

XAVIER'S INSTITUTE
Liberty & Justice for All by Carrie Harris
First Team by Robbie MacNiven
Triptych by Jaleigh Johnson
School of X edited by Gwendolyn Nix

MARVEL MULTIVERSE MISSIONS

YOU ARE (NOT) DEADPOOL

TIM DEDOPULOS

ACONYTE

FOR MARVEL PUBLISHING

VP Production & Special Projects: Jeff Youngquist
Associate Editors, Special Projects: Caitlin O'Connell & Sarah Singer
Manager, Licensed Publishing: Jeremy West
VP, Licensed Publishing: Sven Larsen
SVP Print, Sales & Marketing: David Gabriel
Editor in Chief: C B Cebulski

First published by Aconyte Books in 2022

ISBN 978 1 83908 152 1

Ebook ISBN 978 1 83908 153 8

Cover art by David Nakayama • Interior art by Xteve Abanto
Technical assistance by Jonathan Green • Book design by Nick Tyler

Distributed in North America by Simon & Schuster Inc, New York, USA
Printed in the United States of America
9 8 7 6 5 4 3 2 1

ACONYTE BOOKS

An imprint of Asmodee Entertainment Ltd
Mercury House, Shipstones Business Centre
North Gate, Nottingham NG7 7FN, UK
aconytebooks.com // twitter.com/aconytebooks

OH, HI THERE!

This is an adventure gamebook. If you don't know what that is, maybe flick on through the next few pages for a moment, then head back here...

Yep, that's right, lots of numbered entries. You start at entry **1**, but must then decide which numbered entry to turn to next, according to what the text tells you. You do not just plough straight on to read the next page in order. Not because it's secret, but because it'll be hella confusing, and we don't want that. There's more than enough mayhem incoming as it is.

In this adventure, you take on the role of Deadpool's semi-willing assistant as he blunders through an action-packed mystery. In addition to helping him make decisions, you are going to need to keep track of some stuff as well as rolling some six-sided dice. So grab paper and pencil, or open up a text file, and track down a six-sider or two.

You have three core statistics in this book: **MERC**, **MOUTH**, and **FOCUS**, represented by numbers. *Merc* is physical stuff, *Mouth* is social stuff, and *Focus* is mental stuff. Easy.

They will change a lot over the course of your travels and you'll use them often, so keep a close eye on them. If a stat goes negative, then it makes your rolls and chances of success worse, and in certain circumstances it might even be game over, so try to stay healthy. As a reward for reading this introduction before diving in, ignore what it tells you at entry **35** – instead, start with each of these statistics at 3. It's good to be you.

There is also a whole range of secondary **QUALITIES** you might pick up... {CHAOS}, for example. Qualities are always in {CAPITALS IN CURLY BRACKETS}. Secondary qualities start afresh each new time you play, so if the book tells you to take a Quality you haven't encountered yet, that Quality starts with a score of 1. Keep track of them, because they can seriously change how events unfold. If there's ever a reference to a bonus awarded by a Quality you don't currently have, you don't get that bonus – maybe try to find and acquire that Quality on your adventures.

You'll also find physical **OBJECTS** you can take with you, and they're always marked in [Square Brackets] to show they're special. They might provide bonuses or help with specific situations. Or not. You can have up to **five** objects at once. After that, to take something new, you must drop (cross off) something you already have. Some objects are used up when you employ them, so must be deleted at that point.

During your adventures, you're going to run into **tests**, **fights**, **minigames**, and **puzzles**. They're all clearly labeled. Just follow the instructions at the time. Oh, and there are also some entries with no obvious link leading to them. The clues on how to find them are in the text, mostly. They're worth your while to sniff out.

You can get killed, at least fictionally. Terminal mistakes finish with **The end**. If that happens, your adventure is over. Chalk it up to experience and try again from the start. There are several quite different routes through the book, so you definitely won't see everything in one play-through anyway.

Lastly, as you progress you'll be given ACHIEVEMENTS after certain groovy choices or results. There's a full list at the end of the book. When you're given an achievement, tick it off the list – these are good for multiple play-throughs. If you're reading this in ebook format, you'll have to keep notes somewhere else.

There are also some SUPER-ACHIEVEMENTS listed at the end of the book for finishing the adventure with certain objects or qualities in your possession.

And that's all there is to it. So what are you waiting for? Turn the page!

1

New York City is unusually pleasant this morning. There's some sun, the humidity is low, and no random local has been rude to you for at least five minutes. You're walking across Foley Square, heading for that great little bookstore in Tribeca. A whole week of leisure stretches out ahead of you, and there's a spring in your step for what feels like the first time in months. Even the sight of a red-costumed lunatic lounging along the curving fountain wall like it was some sort of fancy French sofa can't dent your spirits. New York, right?

Then the lunatic points directly at you. "Hey, you!" His voice is peculiar, like someone with guns forced some Hollywood actress to gargle gravel. "Yeah, you! The one with the teeth!"

Despite yourself, that startles you into… well, it's not eye contact exactly, because he's wearing a mask, but you do look into the white fabric in front of his eyes. He instantly rolls off the wall, springs to his feet, and bounds over to you like a puppy. A really big, horrifyingly well-armed puppy. He's got two swords sticking up from behind his shoulders, a pistol holstered on each hip, a knife strapped to one boot, and something you really hope isn't an exotic grenade poking out from one of his belt pouches.

Before you even have a chance to start flinching, he's there, right up in your face. "I do like teeth," he says, as if sharing a secret with his best friend. "They're wonderful,

1

really useful. It's seriously tough without them, and I should know. Agonizing when ripped out."

"Um," you manage. Is he threatening you? "Are you threatening me?"

He takes a half-step back. "What? No! I mean, I don't *think* so. Would you like me to? I'm not judging."

"No!" you reply.

He nods. "Thought so. But are you sure? I can be threatening if that's what you need from me right now. No?" And now he's standing right next to you, pointing at the fountain. "Fine. I like this park. I think it's the way that they put a statue of a prison shiv in the middle of the fountain. It speaks to me, and wow, it hates pigeons."

"I don't think–"

"Don't be so hard on yourself. I'm absolutely convinced you do! That's why I need your help." He looks at you expectantly.

Uh-oh. "My help?"

"OK, let me start from the beginning." He pauses for a moment. "I'm Deadpool. You may have heard of me. I'm kind of a big deal. Fifth spot on the Ranker list of greatest super heroes last time I checked. Would you believe Spider-Man is on the top spot? It's really depressing. What's he got that I haven't – apart from being sticky? Anyhow. It's me. Surprise! I'm on a really important secret mission, given to me by Daredevil. Or was that part secret too? I've got a bad feeling that there is a lot more to it than I know, though. Isn't there always? So I'm worried about everything going wrong. Did I mention that I used to be an Avenger?"

Deadpool. Right. He's not making much sense, but you've heard the name. Some sort of mutant mercenary, but on the good side. Usually.

He pauses for a moment, expectantly. You nod, because that seems safest. "I knew you were smart. So I have to find these alien guns that are flooding the city, but I can't risk being too predictably... me. Not when I don't know what is going on behind the scenes. What if they expect me? So I'm going to do something completely unpredictable instead. That's where you come in."

The day is turning really strange. "Look, um, Deadpool? I'm flattered, I think, but I'm–"

"You're Number Six. Charmed to meet you. We're going to do great things together." He looks over at you. "I'll keep you safe, I promise." For the first time, he actually sounds serious. "I really need your help. If I don't stop these guns getting onto the streets, a lot of people could die. A *lot*. Are you in?"

You think about it for a moment ...

"Sure." Turn to entry **35**.

"Sorry, I can't." Turn to entry **213**.

2

You came here from entry 112 because you failed miserably at throwing severed heads, right? Right? *Right, Ani?* Because if you're just reading straight on from entry 1, you're doing it completely wrong. Please don't do it wrong. It'll get boring really quickly, and then you'll decide we suck, and that would hurt. You're a good person, yeah? Of course you are. So if you did just read on from 1, please go back, make a decision, and do it *right*.

Okay. Phew. They're gone.

It sucks you couldn't land the head-toss, but hey, congratulations for being honest enough to admit it!

Deadpool grumbles, but he can't find any options, so he grabs his swords and hacks his own head clean off. You stare as his body picks his head up, pulls the mask back – oh Lord, the poor, poor man, he is *so* grotesque – and carefully throws it into the scanner. A swooshy metal walkway joins the two platforms, and you walk across. On the other side, Deadpool's body pulls the mask back down then jams the head back on its neck. There's a nasty creak.

"I hope you're grateful," he grumbles. "That's not fun."

Take **-1 MERC** and **+1 {DISCORD}**. ACHIEVEMENT: *Virtue is its Own Reward.*

Through the door on the other side, you find a high-tech control room. Most of the equipment is too intimidating to touch, but there is a normal-looking laptop. Deadpool sits at it.

"Wow, this must be brand new: there are eight thousand free apps that are no possible use to anybody. Ah, there's the browser. It was hiding. Hold on, let me email Weasel." Fifteen minutes later, Deadpool sits back and shakes his head. "This was a total waste of time. I didn't even get a kiss. This conspiracy is national, and the alien wasn't in charge of anything except tech research here. We need to get out of this disappointing pit, go to Boston, and find an Ivy League professor called Hope who runs the Folklore department at Coreham College."

To scout out Coreham College, turn to **287**.

To just go straight there, turn to **148**.

3

You managed to pull off both *One With Everything* and *My Best Me* in the same run? Wow, dear reader. *Wow*. Where, we wonder, did you find the time? Oh, it's certainly possible to do. We admit that. Not very *likely*, but possible.

So if you're here honestly, we sincerely congratulate you on some excellent playing. On the other hand, if you're here, ah, less honestly, we still sincerely congratulate you, this time on some top-notch cheating.

Seriously – for once – we're not convinced you can meaningfully cheat at a single-player experience. If you're having fun, you're doing it right, and don't let different entries tell you otherwise.

ACHIEVEMENT: *Suspiciously Perfect*. You may also take a glittering [Pearl], if you wish.

Now press on to **243**.

4

You enter the mansion. To your surprise, no one appears to hinder you. Huh. The interior is a bit more modern, but still lovely. "They're big on flowers," Deadpool says. "That's a little rococo for my preferences, but I can see the appeal."

You touch a chrysanthemum in a slender vase. It's silk. "Artificial," you say.

He frowns. "You're so judgmental, Six-pack. I just prefer cleaner lines."

As you're exploring, a haughty-looking white guy in an expensive suit comes out of a meditation room and almost blunders into the pair of you. He looks appalled.

Deadpool leaps into action. "Can you keep a secret?" he demands urgently. The man blinks. "Icelandic separatists have taken over. The Rising Shark. Don't Google them, you'll tip them off. They're going to gas everyone at 10 AM, ransom us off, but if we try to evacuate, they'll kill us. I've got to find Broadchurch. Have you seen her?"

"No!"

"Don't tell anyone," Deadpool insists, and gently pushes him back into the room.

The man nods, terrified, already reaching for a cell phone. Note the ACHIEVEMENT: *Come With Me If You Want To Live!*

You've yet to explore the other wings properly. One is themed with oriental dragons, and the other as a koi carp pond.

To try the dragon wing, turn to **89**.
To try the pond wing, turn to **92**.

5

You keep your mouth shut as Deadpool nods happily. "Absolutely!"

As dozens of students crowd round to film everything, the fan – his name is Todd – pulls a wickedly sharp, curved dagger from his bag. Why does he even have that? Deadpool leans forward, and Todd smashes the dagger into Deadpool's left eye socket. Deadpool stifles his groan, bows for the collected screams, then pulls the dagger back out and returns it. "Thanks, Todd! That was refreshing. You really are my best fan." The crowd goes wild, chanting Deadpool's name. Take **+1 MOUTH**.

"This is such an amazing day," Todd babbles. "You have to try the café. It's incredible."

"Do you know where we can find Professor Hope?" you put in.

Todd looks crestfallen. "I'm sorry, it's a big faculty. Try admin or the library? I can take you."

If you want to keep on to the café, turn to **60**.
If you want to try admin, turn to **161**.
If you want to try the library, turn to **299**.

6

The office looks blandly impersonal, more like a high-end Ikea display room than a space anyone actually works in. There's a computer terminal on the desk, a neat pile of paperwork, a jacket on the back of the door, and nothing else. Not a coffee mug in sight.

Make a luck test. Roll one die. On a 5 or more: You see a [Security Pass] clipped to the jacket. You may take it if you like.

To go back to the corridor, turn to **149**.

To head through a side door to the canteen, turn to **290**.

7

Deadpool continues bantering with Weasel, who eventually gives up on trying to concentrate, and says: "Look, there might be a way through from the subway tunnels. I remember a door marked on old maps. Best I can do. Or you can just head to Central Park and improvise."

"Ooh," Deadpool says. "Can I drain the lake?"

"Try not to drain the lake, Wade."

You look at your drink, which smells indescribably nasty. "We should really get going," you say.

If {NO (SUB)WAY} is 1 or more and you want to try to find that route, turn to **182**.

Otherwise, turn to **48**.

8

The bad guys have built a little container fort just off the corner of a couple of roads. There's loads of cover. You watch for a few minutes, and see a steady stream of muscular workers carrying crates down the street to a seedy ship bristling with machine-gun toting mooks. The workers check in there, then carry on to one of several trucks kept under equally heavy guard. One of the trucks is close to full. If you go get the car, you could try following it, or you can send Deadpool in to attack.

To try following the truck, turn to **207**.

To attack the thugs, turn to **21**.

9

Deadpool walks up to the One Family, Inc door and knocks on it politely. A moment later, it opens, and a heavily-armed guard peeks out. "Huh," he says.

Deadpool smashes full-body into the door, flinging it open. The guard is at the top of a staircase that stretches on down, and he has two friends with him. Deadpool draws both of his swords, and darts in between them. Instants later, the blood sprays.

This is a short, ugly fight.

Round one: roll two dice and add your **MERC**. If the total is at least 10, you win. That's it. We told you it was short and ugly. The guards are down either way, but...

If you won, turn to **76**.

If you lost, turn to **297**.

10

You spend a happy hour in Central Park, exploring the landscaping, finishing up with Vista Rock and the Castle. It really is a nice place. Deadpool seems to enjoy it, if the stream of relatively pleasant stories and surprisingly non-horrific memories is anything to go by.

Make an observation test. Roll one die, and add your **FOCUS** to it.

Total of 7 or more and {NO (SUB)WAY} of 1 or more: You overhear a couple of guys worrying about a side door in the subway tunnel. To try that, turn to **182**.

5 or more but without that quality: Deadpool notices some air outlets poking out of the lake. "I could grenade those," he offers. "That would be fun." To blow the lake, turn to **144**.

4 or less: You're just going to have to go in through the front door. Turn to **9**.

11

"How do you feel about heights, Six?" Deadpool asks.

"Um..."

"Perfect. Come on." There's a large department store across the road from the building. Deadpool leads you up to the third floor, and produces an ugly grapple-gun from the bag of tricks you're holding for him. "Ready?"

Before you can say "No!", he kicks out the window and fires the gun down at the Meteorite Building's first floor. A wire trails behind the grapple. Ignoring the screaming customers and staff, he grabs you around the waist and leaps out. Fortunately, he's clipped to the wire, and one horrible and dizzying moment later, you crash through into an office. It hurts, but not so much you can't stand.

Time to see if you're lucky. Roll one die. On a 3 or more: You spot a [Security Pass] on a coat hung behind the door that you may take.

To exit into the corridor, turn to **149**.

To head through a door marked *Canteen*, turn to **290**.

12

Dr Smythe is obviously a bad person. It's not the chemistry equipment, or even the big metal table with worrying straps, that tells you this. It's the hulking great mutated monstrosity. Once a human, it has been twisted into an insectile horror. Savage, over-muscled mantis arms and spiky mandibles accompany huge compound eyes, thin, hairy, claw-footed legs, and a whip-like yellow-black stinger.

It stalks towards you, mandibles clacking. "AXCA," it shrieks, its voice like razors sliding over glass shards. "AXCA!"

Deadpool sighs, and strides over to head it off.

This is a hard fight.

Round one: roll two dice and add your **MERC**. If you have a **[Pointy Stick]**, those eyes are very tempting targets, so add **+3**. If the total is 13 or more, you win the first round.

Round two: roll two dice and add your **MERC**, and another **+3** if you have that **[Pointy Stick]**. If the total is 13 or more, you win the second round.

Poor, doomed Axca. If you lost either round, the fight trashes the room. No loot for you.

If you won both rounds, there's a glittering vial of **[Mutagenic Fluid]** left in the rubble. If you choose to consume it now or in the future, roll one die. 1-2: **MERC**, 3-4: **MOUTH**, 5-6: **FOCUS**. Now roll again, and on 1-3: take **+1** on that stat; on 4-6: take **-1**. Repeat the process twice more.

Now, to return to the corridor, turn to **295**.

To use the door directly to Dr Lundt's lab, turn to **233**.

13

Buzzing alarms sound, and a dozen guards pour out of a white security room to surround you. Both men and women are wearing identical suits, black and expensive, like a scary funeral party. They move gracefully. Deadpool sighs dramatically. "I've always considered violence to be the last resort of idiots and pre-corpses." Take **+1 {DRAGONFIRE}**.

This is a simple intimidation fight.

Round one: roll two dice and add your **MOUTH**. If the total is at least 10, you win the first round.

Round two: roll two dice and add your **MOUTH**, and also **+3** if you won round one. If the total is at least 10, you win the second round.

If you won either round, one of the guards unclips her **[Walkie-Talkie]**, bows, and gives it to you before joining the others in running for the hills of, at a guess, an entirely different continent.

If you want to proceed carefully through the mansion, turn to **92**.

If you want to rush into the security room, turn to **129**.

14

"Wait up, Six," Deadpool says. "This ain't no joke! This really will take you to a completely different reality. You don't want to abandon me, do you? I thought we were buddies." He falls to his knees. "Don't leave me!"

To abandon Deadpool, set {I WAS ONCE A MAN} to 1, grab yourself a copy of *She-Hulk Goes to Murderworld* (all good bookstores, etc), and turn to entry **279** in that book.

To stay in this reality, head deeper into the mines by turning to **224**.

15

The head squelches precisely onto the scanner, face-first. A swooshy metal walkway shoots out to join the two platforms, and you walk across.

ACHIEVEMENT: *The Headmaster.*

Through the door on the other side, you find a high-tech control room. Most of the equipment is too intimidating to touch, but there is a normal-looking laptop computer. Deadpool sits at it.

"Wow, this must be brand new: there are eight thousand free apps that are no possible use to anybody. Ah, there's the browser. It was hiding. Hold on, let me email Weasel." Fifteen minutes later, Deadpool sits back and shakes his head. "Total waste of time. I didn't even get a kiss. This conspiracy is national, and the alien wasn't in charge of anything except tech research here. We need to get out of this disappointing pit, go to Boston, and find an Ivy League professor called Hope, who runs the Folklore department at Coreham College."

To scout out Coreham College first, turn to **287**.

To save time and just go straight there, turn to **148**.

16

A couple of seconds after Deadpool stops hammering on the door, it opens and an angry looking transit official sticks her head out. "Sir..."

Before she can get any further, he yanks the door open hard enough to drag her completely out of the room, and storms inside. There's a desk a few feet inside. As you enter, Deadpool howls in fury, leaps into the air, and smashes down onto the center of the desk. It collapses and shards of computer wreckage go flying. He catches a mug of coffee out of the air, and throws it into a wall. It explodes spectacularly.

"MANAGER!" he shrieks. "NOW!"

Take **+1 MERC**.

The room is silent, the operators cowering behind their equipment banks, the vast data screens flickering noiselessly. Deadpool turns to you and makes a happy finger-guns motion. "Are we sticking with violence, or should we try explaining?"

If you want to stay violent, turn to **264**.

If you want to explain, turn to **250**.

17

Deadpool falls. The flesh-colored horror gestures, and you discover that you are paralyzed. You remain cruelly conscious as you are agonizingly dissected. A period of total blankness follows – a minute? An eon? Hard to know. Then sight flickers back on, and sound, and you discover that you are billions of miles from home, doomed to life eternal as a brain in a jar in an alien library at the very edges of the Sun's grasp.

ACHIEVEMENT: *Me Go Far Away.*

The end.

18

Deadpool drags you out onto the streets of Queens, hunting for a "special friend." After an hour, he spots his quarry: a fried burrito stand called Chimmy's.

"Really?"

"Don't judge by appearances, Sixy. This is serious business. You have no idea how brutal the Taco Wars have been." He heads over to the stand, and brushes his hand over his masked scalp, as if running fingers through his hair. "A three, a four, and a seven please."

The pudgy guy running the stand looks up at him sharply. "Do you want anchovies?"

Deadpool nods decisively. "*All* the anchovies, my friend. All of them."

"Odessa protocol, Wilson?"

"Moscow rules, I think."

The man sighs. "You got it." He reaches into the cart and hands over several hot, greasy packages of deep-fried delight. "Be careful, eh?"

"You too," Deadpool says. Take +2 {CHAOS}.

Now, what is your {GOOD DEED} rating? If it's 1 or more, set {GOOD DEED} to 0 and take -4 {OUT OF TIME}. If it's 0, take -2 {OUT OF TIME} and +2 more {CHAOS}.

Deadpool throws you a chimichanga, and unwraps the end of one of his. "Go on, take a bite. Best in the city." You do, a little nervously. It's... unusual, for sure. Slightly squeaky, yet rather more moist than you anticipated. He leans in. "The secret ingredient," he whispers, "is poutine." You very nearly choke.

Eventually, you get back to the safe-house. Turn to **216**.

19

Hammerhead's eyes flick to where you're crouching behind a marble art stand. "Youse brought me a little mousey, Wilson. Or is it a rat? Sweet of ya. I was getting a little skinny." He brings up his ultramodern Tommygun.

You notice Deadpool's momentary flinch. He starts moving to stand between the two of you. "Joey-baby, you know why you'll never be top dog? You're just another pathetic Russian thug. Sure, you're strong, and you've got that skeleton and enough viciousness to float a kraken, but you don't understand anything. You're as stupid as week-old hamburger. You're a joke, Joe. We all laugh at you – me, Daredevil, Spidey, Kingpin, Doc Ock, the Goblin... Hell, even Juggernaut and the guy I buy papers from on Ninth laugh at you. I pity you, I truly do." Hammerhead pales.

This is the third phase of the final boss fight. Make a goading test – roll one die and add your **MOUTH**.

10 or more: Hammerhead flings his gun aside and leaps at Deadpool, fists already flying.

9 or less: Hammerhead opens up on Deadpool, spraying him up and down with bullets until he runs dry. Oh, it's bad. Take **-3 MERC**.

If your **MERC** is 0 or more, you may turn to **50**.

If your **MERC** is less than zero, you have to surrender. Turn to **30**.

20

You turn to Deadpool. "They must know we're coming. Lets see if we can scare the suits out of the way."

"No problemo, Roku-chan." He pulls out a sword with his left hand and a grenade with his right, and charges the front of the building, screaming what could well be whale-song.

Take **+1 MERC** and **+1 {DRAGONFIRE}**.

The woman disappears almost instantly. You weren't looking, so you don't actually see her vanish, but wow, she's light on her feet. Or a hologram. Or maybe a ghost. Or hey, perhaps… You stop. She's not in the way any more, so whatever.

Deadpool sprints into the building, and you follow.

Make an intimidation test. Roll one die, and add your **MERC** to it.

On a 6 or more: turn to **4**.

5 or less: turn to **13**.

You mention attacking the thugs and he's off, a sword in one hand and a pistol in the other. He's almost there before they even notice him. As the guns come up, he's already leaping. He lands in the middle of them, and the dock erupts.

This is a simple fight.

Round one: roll two dice and add your **MERC**. If the total is at least 9, you win the first round.

Round two: roll two dice and add your **MERC**. If the total is at least 10, you win the second round.

When the smoke clears, Deadpool is standing victorious over a pile of defeated/dismembered bad guys. If you lost either round, a lucky shot tore through his collarbone, so take **-1 MERC**.

The trucks are all long-gone, but one of the thugs had a clipboard with a list of shipment numbers under the heading *Second Family*. There's no address, but it's a firm lead.

Take **+1 {SUSPICIOUS NAME}**. Achievement: *Dock Wolf*.

To follow up on your lead, turn to **86**.

Alternatively, if you haven't already, to try underground routes, turn to **179**.

To try air routes, turn to **91**.

22

Hammerhead is carted off and imprisoned, but his plan rumbles on. Violence engulfs the nation, but it's directionless, and without Hammerhead there to step in and take over, it just keeps rolling. The most savage criminals rise to the top, and even the muggers and street dealers are all toting Chitauri guns now. Thousands die, and many of them were guilty of nothing more than being in the wrong place at the wrong time.

ACHIEVEMENT: *National Chaos.*

Final score: 1 star.

The end.

23

You both sit there weeping for the best part of twenty minutes. Strangely, it helps, reminding you that do you in fact have eyes still, and bodies, and no tentacles.

Take +2 MOUTH for letting your feelings process. You're never getting another moment of sleep without hideous nightmares though.

If you have an [Alien Device], it makes a nasty polyphonic buzzing sound, and the floor swallows you both. Turn to **132**.

Otherwise, you can leave the cupboard by turning to **290**.

24

You are in a long, tiled corridor. There are several doors along its length, with pictures on them to indicate the function of the room, and a sturdy-looking door at the end. No guards are around right now.

Make a luck test. Roll one die. On a 4 or more: Sensors notice you. Take +1 {DRAGONFIRE}.

Now, if your {DRAGONFIRE} is 6 or more, or you just want to ignore the service doors, hurry on to **217**.

To try the "open box of cans" room, turn to **205**.

To try the "filing cabinet" room, turn to **157**.

To try the "beds" room, turn to **173**.

To try the "fish" room, turn to **143**.

25

You pay the old guy a small fortune. He smirks and tells you to use the elevator in the hallway outside to get up to Hammerhead's lair. You shuffle out. Sure enough, there's the elevator. How very bold of you.

ACHIEVEMENT: *Sir Robin*. Take +1 {DISCORD}.

Now, to take five and regain your strength, turn to **159**.

To recap what you're up to, turn to **184**.

To go visit Hammerhead, turn to **271**.

26

You watch in fascinated revulsion as Deadpool and Aleksandr take turns whipping chunks out of the stack. They have to move ridiculously swiftly to avoid toppling the whole thing. Gore spatters everywhere. You think the Russian was going easy on Deadpool at first, but now he's wearing a fierce grin that you're certain Deadpool shares.

Make a horrifying game test!

Roll three dice and add your **MOUTH** and **FOCUS**, as Deadpool attempts to slam an oozing lower thigh from the middle of the stack, whilst simultaneously recounting an unlikely story involving an octopus, three persimmons, and a person who might be a nun, a hairdresser, or both. If you get a total of 17 or more, he did it.

So did he?

Yes: turn to **114**

Or no: turn to **259**.

27

You go through the door on the right into a small, wood-paneled reference library. There's no one here. Most of the books are surprisingly old and staid, like someone decided to just purchase forty square feet of totally respectable book-shelf filler. Heathens.

There are some handwritten notes on a low shelf. If you have a {WET} score of 1 or more, the paper is already ruined. If not, you find a detailed list of personnel guarding the boss today: you may add +1 to all dice rolls in the next fight only.

Heading on through the reference library leads you to a small water cooler area, complete with a breakfast nook, bathrooms, and a frosted glass door to the main office.

To check the breakfast nook, turn to **294**.

To use the bathroom, turn to **90**.

To finally visit the boss, turn to **191**.

28

Crammed in next to Deadpool in the stupid little yellow car as you hurtle back towards New York City, a thought occurs to you. "Why are we in this car, Deadpool?"

"It's all I can afford. I give so much of my money to orphans and pizza delivery folks that at the end of the calendar month, I–"

You shake your head. "No."

"You're right. I could afford better. I just left it too late. I don't expect much out of life, so when they told me that this was the best that they had, I didn't bother–"

"No."

"Fine. I'm worried about the planet, OK? It's only got a 200cc engine, so it's really low emission. That's why the top speed is only three MPH. Sure, it'll take us a couple of months longer, but that's a small price to pay for keeping Greta happy. I'd do anything for that young–"

"No."

He sighs, suddenly sad again. "You remind me of an old friend. I thought it would be funny, okay?"

"And is it?"

"No. It sucks."

You nod. "Yeah."

If your {CHAOS} is 15 or more, take the ACHIEVEMENT: *You* Have *Been Naughty*.

Now, if your {CHAOS} is 5 or more, or you have {NO (SUB)WAY} or {CENTRAL CRATER} at 1 or – somehow – more, then turn to **44**.

If you don't have any of those things, take the ACHIEVEMENT: *Low Profile*, then turn to **138**.

29

The pilot sets off after the unmarked black helicopter, which is heading north. For a minute or two, you gain on it without any problems. Then it apparently notices you, because it speeds up and whips behind a tall building. Mr Davies curses, and tries to follow it.

It's time for a chase minigame!

Round 1: Roll one die, and add your **FOCUS**.

On a 6 or more: Take **+2** next round.

Get 5 or less: Take **-1** next round.

Round 2: Roll one die, and add your **FOCUS**, and last round's adjustment.

6 or more: turn to **79**.

5 or less: turn to **101**.

30

Deadpool slumps to his knees, beaten.

How much damage did you do to Hammerhead's plans? Add up your {CASH DOWN}, {WEAPONS DOWN}, and {NAMES DOWN}, if any. What's the total?

If it's 6 or more: Turn to **286**.

5 or less: Turn to **58**.

31

Using your cell phone for light, you pick your way along the tunnel. After a twisty, turny minute or so, it stops. There's a small table with a note and a plate.

The note says: *Really?*

The plate holds a couple of [Cookies] you can take, if you trust random maze cookies. They have chocolate chips. You hope it's chocolate.

To return to the junction and go left, turn to **276**.

To return to the junction and go straight ahead, turn to **117**.

32

The shed door now before you is lighter than it should be, almost like a puff of smoke. Off past it, you can see a crumbling old hut, and a boxy brick storage building squats unpleasantly within a nest of weeds. Inside, there's a jumble of strange, decaying electromechanical junk.

Oddly, much of the detritus is floating a couple of feet in the air.

You push on in to the shed, the trash parting around you. Deadpool carefully pokes a piece, sending it banging into another chunk, and the resulting tangle spins into an old refrigerator and clunks to a stop. "Neat," he says.

In one corner, there are some reasonably clean [UFO Parts] that you may take.

To try the storage building, go to **137**.

To check out the crumbling hut, go to **203**.

33

You crawl back to consciousness, head pounding. You discover you're tied very firmly to an office chair. Deadpool's next to you, in a chair of his own. The pair of you are in what looks to be a secure art vault. Mostly they are beautiful paintings of threatening, somewhat retro-looking city streets, though you also spot some vintage movie posters – *Dr Mabuse, Belphégor, Underworld* – and a couple of Soviet "For sure, Ivan, hard work is truly great!" propaganda pieces. It's an interesting selection.

A polite cough draws your attention to a man with arms like oaks and legs like beer barrels. He's in his late thirties at a guess, with a buzz cut and high cheekbones. He's wearing a gorgeous black smoking jacket with gold silk trim over a thread-of-gold shirt and deep green pants that work surprisingly well with it.

"Mighty Deadpool! Is honor." Yes, he has a strong

Russian accent. "Have always wanted to meet you. And little companion. Hello, little companion. Name is Aleksandr Kuznetsov, but please, call me Jengarm."

"Hi Alex," Deadpool says. "Meet Number Six. Is that a Derek Rose?"

"Please, friend Deadpool. Is no need for mockery. Is Gieves and Hawkes, of course."

"I totally understand. You have a lot to compensate for."

"I wonder are you good as advertised. Have longed to test skills for years now."

"Untie me, and you'll find out exactly how good I am."

"Hope so, yes. Want you to play me at balance game. Win, I help. Lose, we fight instead. Yes?"

Deadpool looks over to you. It's got to be worth a try. You nod.

"Let's play, Comrade Jengarm," Deadpool says.

The Russian smiles broadly. "Delightful! Is very great day." He claps, once. Deadpool's ropes fall away and he stands as a pair of unhappy security guards shuffle into view. They're carrying a heavy table covered in a thick rubber mat, and on the mat is a swaying tower of freshly-severed human limb segments. These are stacked three to a level, each layer perpendicular to the one below. Blood is oozing down the whole affair, and it smells like a butcher's nightmares. "You see why name, yes?" he asks proudly. "Is leg also. Less waste. But Jengarmleg not so... *kratkiy*. Snappy."

Make a horrifying game test!

Round 1: Roll two dice and add your **MERC** and **FOCUS**,

as Deadpool yanks a chunk of forearm from near the top of the stack. On a 13 or more: you win round one.

Round 2: Roll two dice and add your **MERC** and **FOCUS**. If you won round 1, add **+2** as a bonus. On a 13 or more: you win round two.

Did you win round two?

Yes: turn to **26**.

No: turn to **259**.

34

A couple of seconds after Deadpool stops hammering on the door, it opens and an angry-looking transit official sticks her head out. "Sir, I..." Her brain catches up with the message her eyes are screaming to her, and the rest of her sentence vanishes.

"Hi!" Deadpool says. "I'm Deadpool. You need to let us in to the control room."

Her face turns suspicious. "I'm sorry, but–"

"The details are classified, but I'm working with Daredevil, investigating a terror plot. We believe a hostile force is using your network to smuggle incredibly dangerous weapons into the city. We need to speak to your controller."

The woman nods, slowly. "I'll call her. I guess you should come in."

Take **+1 FOCUS**.

The control room is impressive. The walls are covered with technical data screens, and the floor area holds row after row of computer stations, equipment banks, and other large electronic bits. A dozen operators or more are working here, although most of them are looking over at you right now. Deadpool waves at them, and they immediately look away. Then he turns to you. "The controller will be here soon, Xis. Are we staying honest, or should I embellish?"

If you want to keep being honest, turn to **250**.

If you want to try lying, turn to **180**.

35

A lot of people are in danger, and Deadpool did promise he could keep you safe. How can you refuse? "Sure. I'm in. What do we have to do?"

"I'm so glad you asked me that. We have to find the guns. It'll be a piece of cake, Daredevil said." He pauses for a moment. "I like cake."

"Uh–"

"Sure, sure. Don't worry, Number Six. I won't let you starve. That's a horrible way to die. You trust me, right? Great. Now first, we need to take stock. Go on, take a good, long look at me. Run your eyes all over me, like a dog chasing a drone around a park. What do you see?"

Now, this is where you – that's *you* you, dear reader – get to determine the starting statistics for your team of Deadpool and Number Six. There are three stats, which you'd know if you'd read the introduction, but we're not bitter that you skipped it. Just wanted to get to the fun stuff, right?

The stats are **MERC**, **MOUTH**, and **FOCUS**.

Merc represents Deadpool's talent for violence and other physical feats, like bending iron bars or drinking a *really* spicy sauce, like millions of Scovilles. Also surviving the morning after that sauce. Seriously, don't drink bottles of chilli sauce. It's not good for you.

Mouth represents Deadpool's social skills, which span the whole range from being confusing to being annoying. Okay, fine, he can also be really baffling, frightening, and even – occasionally – charming, when the moon is full. No, Deadpool is absolutely not a Were-Princess. We deny that completely. You didn't hear it from us.

Focus, finally, is the team's awareness, concentration, and general capacity to pay attention. This is where Number Six really shines. Hopefully. Focusing is not Deadpool's strong suit.

All three stats begin at 2, but you can add one point to any *one* of them. Over the course of the adventure, these stats will change, increasing or decreasing according to the choices that you make and the consequences you bring down upon yourself. They will help you succeed in challenges, specifically *tests* and *fights*.

You'll need to keep track of these stats. We recommend some paper and a pencil, but you may prefer a blank text doc, or a wall and a crayon, maybe a tattoo gun and a very open-minded friend, whatever suits. You'll also need a couple of dice, or some other way of generating random numbers from 1 to 6, or multiples thereof.

As you play, you'll pick up some secondary qualities. They're like stats, so they represent a score, but they're a lot more varied and differ from game to game. Secondary qualities are always mentioned in {CURLY BRACKETS}. If you're told to increase a secondary quality and you don't already have a score in it, it starts at zero.

So, for example, *if* you're told that you're getting +1 {KUMQUAT}, your {KUMQUAT} goes from 0 to 1. Note that you will never, *ever* be told that you are getting +1 {KUMQUAT}. Not by us. Horrid things. Ugh.

Anyway, for now, you just have **MERC**, **MOUTH**, and **FOCUS**, and nothing else. Definitely zero {KUMQUAT}. Two of the three stats are at 2, and the third is at 3. Right? Right. Now back to the action…

Deadpool raises an eyebrow at you. "Whoa there, Six. Calm down. What's important is finding how these Chitauri guns are being smuggled into the city."

"Chitauri?"

"Exactly. Come one!" He heads across the park to Centre Street, and leads you to a tiny, malformed yellow car. "This is us." He proceeds to get in, levering himself behind the wheel somehow. Did he just dislocate a rib to fit in there?

As you fold yourself into the minuscule compartment next to him, he glances at you. "It's a rental, OK? It's a car though. Officially. It's even good for the planet, because the engine is smaller than the one on my smoothie blender. If you prefer, I know a guy who can get us some horses."

How about space to move my knees away from my chin? you think. "It's fine."

He looks at you for a moment, arms splayed so he can hold the wheel. "Aww. Anyhow, there's three ways to smuggle things into a place – through the air, along the surface, or under the ground. Unless they're using nightmarish alien dimensions, but we should leave those for plan B. Where should we start?"

ACHIEVEMENT: *But Thou Must!*

(Yay! Achievements! How modern! When you get an achievement for the first time, you can mark it off the list at the very back at this book, or if you're experiencing this in ebook format, uh, just write it in your daily journal, OK?)

To search the skies, turn to entry **91**.

To search the surface, turn to **43**.

To search below the ground, turn to **179**.

36

You lose sight of the truck for a moment, but you catch it as it heads onto the freeway.

"Grab the wheel," Deadpool says.

Suddenly he's climbing onto you and shoving you over. The little car veers wildly, and horns blare at you, but somehow you keep from crashing. The car has almost stopped by the time you're wedged in enough to control it, but you gamely set off after the truck.

"Bring me alongside," Deadpool says. "A long side. That's a silly word. You can totally be alongside a short side, but I'd never say 'bring me ashortside.' That would just be embarrassing."

He keeps on in this vein, but you're driving. The truck has slowed to avoid suspicion, and as you're crossing a bridge, you get near the truck driver's door.

Deadpool squeezes out and jumps onto the truck. His sword flashes, and the truck's tire explodes. It careens wildly towards the bridge railing, then plummets down into the river. You watch it fall in horror, then realize Deadpool is clinging to the railing, dangling the driver over the river. Everything screeches to a halt.

The truck driver is shrieking. Below him, familiar crates are sinking into the river.

"Wait!" the driver shouts. "Please! I'm only on a short-term contract!"

"Where do the boxes go?" Deadpool demands.

"A warehouse. Changes every time." Apparently

Deadpool's grip loosens for a moment, because the guy shrieks again. "Wait, damn it! I heard a name. *Second Family*. That's who they're going to. That's all I know, I swear!"

Deadpool hauls the driver back up onto the sidewalk, and the man collapses sobbing.

ACHIEVEMENT: *Dock Wolf*.

Take +1 {SUSPICIOUS NAME}.

To follow up on your lead, turn to **86**.

Or, if you haven't already:

To try underground routes, turn to **179**.

To try air routes, turn to **91**.

37

Lifeguard, whose real name is Heather Cameron, has been part of the X-Men, the Utopian X-Men, X-Corporation, and the X-treme X-Men. She can manifest whatever is needed to save a life around her, and has been seen living in Krakoa. She is not the odd one out. Sorry.

Go back to **216**.

38

The computer equipment in this room is extremely high-tech, possibly even suspiciously so. "Don't worry," Deadpool says, immediately making you worry. "I can do this."

He phones Weasel, and with his help, tries to crack into the accounts.

If you are carrying **[UFO Parts]**, the computers mysteriously let Deadpool run rampant without even logging in. Take **+3** {CASH DOWN} and **+2** {FLUSH}.

Otherwise, make a hacking test. Roll one die, and add your **FOCUS**, and your {NET OPS} and {TERRIFYING WEASEL}, if any. If you have a **[Sparkling Icosahedron]**, add **+2** to the total.

Score an 8 or more: Take **+3** {CASH DOWN} and **+1** {FLUSH}.

On a 5-7: Take **+2** {CASH DOWN}.

If it's 4 or less: Take **+1** {CASH DOWN} and **+2** {CHAOS} as Deadpool cackles and crashes Wall Street.

Now head back to the safe-house by turning to **216**.

39

Deadpool leads you to an apartment tower with an accessible fire-escape. The pair of you climb up it to the roof. You're not really surprised that no one takes any notice – this is New York, after all – but none of the people whose apartments you schlep past even look up. When you get to the low wall surrounding the edge, Deadpool hops up onto it and squats down on his haunches to stare broodily out over the city. You stay a good couple of feet back, and watch for several minutes as he stares out, looking all moody and artistic.

Take **+2 FOCUS** and **+1** {AWARE}.

"The city is a living thing," he says, his voice gruff and mournful. "She has moods, whims... Scrofula. Maybe wallabies? They get everywhere, the bouncy little... Uh, scamps. Oh hey, look, I've eaten at that place. Really good sushi."

"Um–"

He sighs, and hops back off the wall. "I don't know. It works for Daredevil. Maybe he's like a moth, except blind. It's a mystery. Let's go."

As you leave, you spot a place where some kids have been playing detective. You may take one of either a [Magnifying Glass] or a [Stethoscope] with you.

You go back to the safe-house. Turn to **216**.

40

"I just can't." You shrug uncomfortably. "I'm sorry, but I'm not the person you're looking for."

"Fine," Deadpool says. He glares at the statue. "I really should know better than to trust a gigantic shiv stuck into a fountain. Good luck, Number Six. I hope you make it." He turns and slouches off across the park and down Lafayette.

You push the strange encounter out of your mind, and continue on your way to Tribeca.

ACHIEVEMENT: *Be Seeing You.*

(Yay! Achievements! How modern! When you get an achievement for the first time, you can mark it off the list at the back at this book, or if you're reading this as an ebook, write it in your diary?)

The end.

41

Deadpool collapses, a big, smoking hole where his face really rather ought to be. The old man smirks, presses a button, and then turns the gun on you as yellow-suited guards rush in.

You didn't even make it to Hammerhead. How depressing.

ACHIEVEMENT: *The Final Hurdle.*

The end.

42

There's a Tommy-gun near to your feet. You pry the severed hand off it, then start firing. Deadpool never sees it coming. You pump bullet after bullet into his head, and keep going even when Hammerhead recovers and stands up, watching you.

"He just will *not* shut up," you grate out.

Hammerhead nods thoughtfully. "I gots some openings in my crew now, Ratty, and I like ya style. Youse in?"

"Abso*lute*ly, boss," you say.

Despite the hiccups you've inflicted, with Hammerhead in place the plan goes off flawlessly. Six months later, Kingpin, Doc Ock, Eduardo Lobo, and even Mister Negative are all deposed. You're running the West Coast, living like a monarch. An evil, evil monarch. So, uh, like most monarchs. America slides into despair as Hammerhead tightens his grip, but that just makes your victory all the sweeter.

Deadpool's still getting tortured to a horrible demise six

or more times a day. There's no way he'll ever escape, so you're completely and totally safe. Oh yes.

ACHIEVEMENT: *Turncoat.*

FINAL SCORE: As many stars as you want. All the stars.

The end.

43

"Smuggling large shipments of weapons sounds easiest using normal transportation methods," you say.

"Teleporting into Nate's abdomen? I like the way you're thinking, but he's dead. You don't want to teleport guns into Cable's corpse. It'd be hilarious, but you'd get all sorts of muck into them, and they might react with some of his implants in unpredictable ways, and anyway, he might just be ash now for all I know. I went to his funeral. If there was a funeral. Maybe I sent flowers. Or a bomb."

"What about the port?" you quickly say the moment he pauses.

"I never bombed the port." He sounds hurt. "Damn. Now I feel left out. When did you get to bomb the port, Six? You've got hidden depths."

"Maybe the smugglers are there."

"Yeah, a few bombs wouldn't put these guys off! Good thinking. Let's do it."

The sad little car puffs into action and lurches forward like it's got vehicular arthritis. Deadpool's driving style is horrifying, but somehow you don't crash, and to your great sorrow, he drives to Jersey.

A half-hour later, you park up at the Red Hook Container Terminal. It's a horror – ugly concrete boxes, gigantic industrial cranes, and an ever-sprawling maze of shipping containers. The rentacop on the gates takes one look at the pair of you and hides, buzzing the door open as you approach.

You wander around the port for a few minutes. Wow, that's a lot of containers, and Deadpool seems determined to put a name to the exact shade of each one.

"Taupe. Puce. Bilious Green. Ooh, look, Greased Brains!"

You glance over just in case, but no, it's another container. "Maybe we should try something else?" you suggest.

"Absolutamentely, Seis. What did you have in mind?"

If you want to find someone to bribe, turn to **141**.

If you want to scout from a high spot, turn to **193**.

If you want to find the harbormaster, turn to **200**.

44

You're in Deadpool's Yellow Mistake, heading over the Whitestone Bridge towards a safe-house he claims to have in Bushwick, a cool Hispanic district in Brooklyn, when someone knocks on the window. Outside, easily matching your pace, is a huge guy wearing red metal-effect cycle gear, riding an equally huge motorbike. He waves for Deadpool to pull over. You stop, and immediately car horns start blaring as other drivers are forced to acknowledge the existence of something outside themselves. The motorcycle stops behind you as the pair of you get out.

Oh. It's not cycle gear, that weird tapering dome isn't a bike helmet, and he's not just huge, he looks like a force of nature. You've seen a lot of very burly men and women in the last day or so, but this one just redrew the boundaries. Juggernaut stomps over to meet you. He does not look happy.

"Wilson, you freak. What in the six freaking hells are you up to? Do you have any idea how much trouble you caused? You got exactly one chance to explain before I tear your head off and pound it into mush."

If you try explaining, turn to **288**.

If you start a fight, turn to **167**.

45

You decide to try the jagged path.

"You like rough?" Deadpool asks. "I'm surprised, Sixford. Rough is always relative though. Sandpaper is velvety smooth compared to a cheese grater, if you get my meaning. And a tunnel-borer, wow, that's another level entirely. Just completely different."

"Is this a euphemism?"

"What?"

A loud rumble interrupts your conversation, thankfully, then the roof of the passage is collapsing in on you.

Make an awareness test. Roll one die, and add your **FOCUS** to it.

Score 7 or more: You manage to leap ahead of the fall.

Make 5-6: You leap aside, but have to dig clear. Take **+1 {STUCK FOR A TIME}**.

On 4 or less: Deadpool is clobbered. Take **+1 {STUCK FOR A TIME}** and **-2 MERC**.

Now, on the other side is a junction. The glow leads onwards, but there's a strong draft blowing from another passage.

To follow the glow, turn to **118**.

To follow the draft, turn to **127**.

46

Time has run out. Now you have to get moving. The Meteorite Building awaits. There's just a few things to check first.

If you have {UNLIKELY ALLY} of 1, add **+1** to either {CASH DOWN}, {NAMES DOWN}, {WEAPONS DOWN}, or {RESOURCEFUL}, to reflect Jengarm helping behind the scenes.

If you have {CASINO OUTRAGE} of 3 or more, your supposedly safe storage unit is attacked by a pack of machine-gun wielding Mafia soldiers sent by their furious boss.

This is a moderately tricky fight.

Round one: roll two dice and add your **MERC**. If the total is at least 11, you win the first round.

Round two: roll two dice and add your **MERC**. If the total is at least 11, you win the second round.

Round three: roll two dice and add your **MERC**. If the total is at least 10, you win the third round.

The soldiers are all dead by the end of the fight, but how one-sided was it?

If you won at least two rounds, take **+1 MOUTH** in smugness.

If you lost at least two rounds, take **-2 MOUTH** in humiliation.

And now, if you have at least 1 in each of {CASH DOWN}, {NAMES DOWN}, {WEAPONS DOWN}, and {RESOURCEFUL}, turn to **225**.

If you have at least 1 in each of {TOOLED UP}, {ZANY}, {FEELING GOOD}, {AWARE}, and {FLUSH}, turn to **293**.

If you're, um, still here, turn instead to **243**.

47

You take a path leading away from the woman and stroll around until you see a side door. It's guarded, but the guy ignores you. A short distance away, there's a shed of gardening equipment. You go round the side of it, out of sight. "Got a lighter?" you ask.

"Do I ever." Deadpool pulls out a colorful little plastic thing and starts trying to burn the side of the shed.

Take **+1 FOCUS**. There's a [Large Metal Block] here – but it needs two inventory slots if you want to take it.

It takes a minute, but the fire begins to catch. You walk off, pretending to chat. Eventually the guard curses and dashes over to the shed. You saunter into the building.

Make a distraction test. Roll one die, and add your **FOCUS** to it.

Score 5 or more: turn to **4**.

Make 4 or less: turn to **13**.

48

Central Park looks lovely this afternoon, full of relaxed people having a nice time in this green oasis in the middle of the city. Poor fools. You suspect their day is going to get a lot more stressful any moment. You lead Deadpool to the spectacular tiled arcade of Bethesda Terrace. It's difficult imagining someone getting permission to put a door in, but there it is, at the back, facing the fountain. It's a modest glass door, frosted and reasonably appealing, but still, it must have taken some serious sway. ONE FAMILY, INC is stenciled on it.

"Glass smashes," Deadpool says.

"I'm not sure–"

"It does, I promise. Really easily. I've done it myself."

Hmm.

If you want to smash your way in, turn to **9**.

If you want to try a distraction, turn to **188**.

If you want to search this part of the park for options, turn to **10**.

49

The locker buzzes rudely at you, and the lights turn red. "Nice work, Six-pest. Really great."

Deadpool's fist flashes past your face, and the locker door crumples. There's one item inside, a note saying that last Thursday's password for the One Family, Inc facility on Bethesda Terrace Arcade is *Swordfish*. Of course it is.

Deadpool grabs the note. "One is more important than Second. But shouldn't it be First? That's sloppy. Although First Family would sound like the president was crooked. Huh. Can you imagine? Thank the Lord that this is America." He winks at you, incredibly obviously.

If you want to research One Family, Inc, turn to **175**.

If you'd rather head straight over to Central Park, turn to **48**.

50

Hammerhead and Deadpool tear into each other, mano a mano, shouting incoherently. Hammerhead is so monstrously strong that every missed punch is another hole in the marble, but he's slow. Deadpool is athletic and shrugs off broken bones, but his opponent has a super-strong adamantium skeleton. They wreck each other back and forth, Hammerhead clobbering like a truck, Deadpool darting about and aiming for soft tissue.

This is the fourth phase of the final boss fight.

Round one: roll two dice and add your **MERC** and **FOCUS**. If the total is at least 18, you win the first round.

Round two: roll two dice and add your **MERC** and **FOCUS**. If the total is at least 18, you win the second round.

Round three: roll two dice and add your **MERC** and **FOCUS**. If the total is at least 17, you win the third round.

Round four: roll two dice and add your **MERC** and **FOCUS**. If the total is at least 17, you win the fourth round.

Round five: roll two dice and add your **MERC** and **FOCUS**. If the total is at least 16, you win the fifth round.

If you won at least three rounds, turn to **211**.

If you lost three rounds or more, turn to **30**.

51

You come down into a claustrophobic network of concrete steam tunnels. Guards and office types bustle back and forth in the dimness, even the occasional person in overalls, but there's no one near you.

Test your luck. Roll one die.

On a 4-6: Systems flag up possible intruders. Take **+1 {CENTRAL ALERT}**.

If you roll 1-3: Someone spots you as they pass and calls it in. Take **+2 {CENTRAL ALERT}**.

Grubby signs on the tunnel walls point towards administration one way and storage the other. "Are you an office Christmas party or an illegal warehouse rave?" Deadpool asks.

If you want to try admin, turn to **281**.

If you want to try storage, turn to **282**.

52

You are – and we cannot stress this enough – standing with Deadpool on the edge of a bottomless pit of eldritch doooooom, thinking about flinging yourselves in. This is an *extremely* bad idea. As you waver, the hungry whispers increase their intensity, desperate for you to succumb.

To really jump, go to **162**.

To snap out of it, follow the glow to **118**.

53

You gesture at the door. "Let's do this."

"Now you're talking sense," Deadpool says.

"That's worrying."

"Isn't it though?" He pulls out his guns, and marches through the doors of the Meteorite Building and into the lobby. You hang back and watch as the horde of blue-suited guards open fire. Huh. Good soundproofing.

Take **+1 {WARNED}**.

This is a very hard fight.

In round one: roll two dice and add your **MERC** and your **{CASH DOWN}** – hirelings do expect payment. If the total is at least 17, you win the first round.

Round two: roll two dice and add your **MERC** and your **{CASH DOWN}**. If the total is at least 17, you win the second round.

Round three: roll three dice and add your **MERC** and your **{CASH DOWN}**. If the total is at least 20, you win the third round.

Eventually, Deadpool is the only one standing, and it's reasonably safe to go in, so you can discover how much punishment he took.

If you won every round, take **-1 MERC**. If you lost any rounds, take **-3 MERC**.

As you pick your way over the blue slaughter, you notice that many of the guards are wearing a **[Security Pass]**. You can take one with you, if you want – five items maximum though, remember?

If you want to use the elevators, turn to **249**.

If you would rather take the stairs, turn to **171**.

54

"You won't regret this," Deadpool says, excitedly scrawling an address label. "The Chimichanga Wars are getting really brutal, and Gabriel has the best truck on the entire eastern seaboard. Now he'll be able to blow the opposition completely away."

You just gave a crate of super villain weapons to a street-food vendor. Yay?

Take **+1 {CHAOS}** and **+1 {GOOD DEEDS}**.

If you go on to the command suite, turn to **232**.

If you stay in Shipping, turn to **255**.

55

At your suggestion, Deadpool presses the button. "I love pressing big red buttons like this," he says. "It's like a murder mystery, except you don't know what's going to happen. Do you think we just nuked Tulsa?"

"Maybe," you say. "The door certainly didn't open."

The pair of you look at it. "No," he agrees. "It didn't."

Then the door opens. A huge pack of guards floods out – thirty or more.

This is a hard fight. Take **+1 {ROLLING STONE}**.

Round one: roll two dice and add your **MERC**. If the total is at least 10, you win the first round.

Round two: roll two dice and add your **FOCUS**. If the total is at least 9, you win the second round.

In round three: roll two dice and add your **MERC**. If the total is at least 10, you win the third round.

If you won all three rounds, turn to **247**.

If you lost any rounds, turn to **109**.

56

You notice that one of the downed guards has an oddly glittering object around his neck. Most impressive! ACHIEVEMENT: *Secret Hunter Four.*

You take the object, and see that it is a pendant in the shape of a surprisingly accurate ant's head. It's grotesque and, strangely, it is glowing with a soft red light.

Deadpool looks over at it, and you'd swear it just twitched. "What's that?" He takes the pendant from you. It emits a chittering sound, flashes brightly, and dissolves into the fabric covering his hand.

"I-must-serve-the-queen," says Deadpool, his voice like ice. You flinch. "Nah, only joking."

Take **+1** Mouth, **+1** Merc, **+1** Focus, and **+1** {**CHAOS**}.

Now turn to entry **124**.

57

Brattleboro is a beautiful little town in the southeast corner of Vermont. Stately red brick buildings dominate the downtown area, which feels calm and creative. It's almost as if the place has been caught slightly out of time. Deeply-wooded hills loom up behind it, oddly threatening. A natural hiding place for werewolves, or worse things.

As you pass through the town and along the West River, the countryside becomes less tame, less reassuring. The road narrows, until it's little more than a thread picking its way through the hills, the thick forests crowding in as if hungry.

Deadpool must catch a sense of your mood, because he glances over and shrugs. "Never met a tree I couldn't outrun." You chuckle at that, and the route seems a bit less oppressive. "Yeah," he says. "It's not the trees, it's what they're hiding." Then he spots a sparrow.

You turn onto a smaller road, and then again, a half hour later, onto a barely-paved track that winds up through wooden cliffs to end, eventually, at a towering wire fence and a pair of heavy metal gates. The gates have been welded shut. You might be able to climb them, or you could try heading down the side, between the forest and the fence, and see if you can find an easier way in.

If you want to climb the gates, turn to **260**.

If you want to push down the side, turn to **74**.

58

Hammerhead descends on Deadpool like an earthquake, pounding and pounding until there's nothing left but horribly-twitching meat paste. "Pulls yaself together, Wilson. Plenty more where that came from." He turns to you. "And you, rat..." He slams you across the room into a wall. Agony blazes. You're barely aware he's raising a foot above your head. Then the lights go out.

You won't know anything about the huge wave of deaths that shock the nation, or Hammerhead's deposing of Kingpin and Doc Ock, or the way that the entire country gets nastier and nastier over the following years as it slides into a criminal kakistocracy. Because you're already dead.

ACHIEVEMENT: *That Went Well.*

FINAL SCORE: No stars.

The end.

59

Abyss was an alien servitor created by the Builders, the universe's oldest race. She was inducted into the Avengers on the recommendation of Captain Universe, and gave her life to help hold back an incursion of Beyonders from the non-space outside Omniverse. She was never affiliated with the X-Men, which makes her the odd one out. Well done! Take +1 {PUZZLER} and +1 FOCUS.

The deciphered clues lead you and Deadpool to a

brownstone in a harmless-looking residential district. The courier, who calls themselves Talon Minor, has a drop to make. You wait down the road a bit, keeping watch on the building. In a short time, they exit the building, dressed like a perfectly normal office drone. You follow.

Deadpool is not very good at the whole unnoticeable thing, and Talon Minor spots you almost immediately. They take off at high speed.

Make a chase test. Roll one die and add your **MERC**.

If you score 6 or more, turn to **210**.

On 5 or less, you lose them. Turn to **216**.

60

In fairness to Todd, he's right. The café is amazing. There are two separate professional coffee concessions, plus a gelato stand, a smoothie bar, an alcohol-free cocktail bar, several top-end restaurant operations, and a whole flotilla of comfy sofas. By the time you walk in, the place is completely crowded with fans. Deadpool is in his element, soaking up the adulation, talking nonsense to anyone and everyone, and having a wonderful time.

Take **+1** Merc, and **+1** {GUARDS, GUARDS}.

A breathless young woman offers Deadpool a very fancy [Crystal Monocle] as a gift. It gives you **+2 FOCUS** for as long as it is in your inventory.

Before long, the crowd are begging for a repeat performance of Deadpool's healing factor. Are you going to let him show off?

If yes, take **+2 MOUTH**, **-1 MERC**, and **+1 {CHAOS}**.

If no, take **+2 FOCUS**, **-1 MOUTH**, and **+1 {DISCORD}**.

Eventually, you manage to persuade Deadpool to ask Todd to help you find the professor.

If you want to try Admin, turn to **161**.

If you want to try the library, turn to **299**.

61

Forearm, whose truly incredible alias disguises his real name of Michael McCain, spent most of his career fighting the X-Men, but was eventually welcomed into Professor X, Magneto, and Moira X's new mutant nation, Krakoa. Since then, he's joined S.W.O.R.D and worked with Magik, Colossus's sister. He is not the odd one out. Sorry.

Go back to **216**.

62

As the light dies away, you realize that you're underground. It's too regular to be a natural cave, and there's a phosphorescence to the walls that lights everything up with a sea-green glow. Deadpool's costume looks entirely black in this light. It's not an improvement.

Take **+1 {PUZZLER}**.

"So I guess we're in a maze of twisty passages that are all alike," Deadpool says. You look around more carefully. He's not wrong. There are tunnels leading off to the left, the right, and straight ahead, and there's nothing to tell them apart – except that the one to the left is lit by the green phosphorescence, while the other two are pitch black.

To go left, turn to **276**.

To go right, turn to **31**.

To go straight ahead, turn to **117**.

63

You shouldn't be here. You know that as well as we do. There's no entry anywhere in this book that leads here. You are, not to put too fine point on it, *cheating*.

Well, fine. If you want to cheat, then cheat. We can't stop you, so we might as well help. If you can't beat them, join them, right?

Take this **[Laser Sword]**. It makes cool noises, it doesn't use an inventory space, and while you have it, you automatically win every round of every fight.

ACHIEVEMENT: *Secret Hunter Five* and ACHIEVEMENT: *Swooshy*.

Now return to wherever you came from, and let us never speak of this again.

64

Deadpool is flung across the room, his torso chopped open from neck to navel, innards trailing through the air behind him. If he's not dead, he's doing a very good impersonation. You've been huddling behind a large, ugly pot-plant, so you don't see Palmetto approaching, Chitauri gun at the ready.

Deadpool groans. "Now I'm going to need another one," he says weakly and everything goes black.

ACHIEVEMENT: *The Replacements*.

The end.

65

You come out of the clanging maze via a door, that leads into the back of a plush office. Unlike most of the offices in this building, this one actually looks used. You're between a bookcase and a filing cabinet, behind and to one side of an attractive teak desk which holds a pricy computer, several horrible executive toys, an actual telephone, a bunch of paperwork, and a mug of slightly-steaming coffee. Past the desk is a big, carpeted space with a sofa nook, several certificates, various items of art, and a couple of uncomfortable guest chairs.

"What the holy Moses are you chuckleheads doing here?" a voice demands in a thick Al Capone accent. You look past the bookcase to a big leather office chair and the red-suited guy sitting in it. He's older, maybe early sixties, and he looks like a scrawny old ranch-hand, all gristle, bone, and spite.

"Oh, we're just passing through," Deadpool says cheerfully.

"Is that so? Well I don't take kindly to tourists, see." He stands up. That bulge in his jacket is definitely a big gun.

If you have {FLUSH} of 2 or more, you can bribe him to let you go peacefully. Turn directly to **25**.

Otherwise, he pulls out a really long .45, and this is a hard sub-boss fight.

Round one: roll three dice and add your **MOUTH**, and if you have any, your {WEAPONS DOWN}. Then subtract your {WARNED}. If the total is at least 16, you win the first round.

Round two: roll three dice and add your **MERC**, and if you have any, your {WEAPONS DOWN}. Then subtract your {WARNED}. If the total is at least 15, you win the second round.

Round three: roll three dice and add your **FOCUS**, and if you have any, your {WEAPONS DOWN}. Then subtract your {WARNED}. If the total is at least 17, you win the third round.

If you lose two or more rounds, go straight to **41**.

Otherwise, take -1 {WARNED} and the ACHIEVEMENT: *Appetiser*.

To take five, turn to **159**.

To head up to Hammerhead's Lair for the main event, turn to **271**.

66

You've followed Talon Minor through the mall and into the changing rooms of a gym. They're in here somewhere, but there are a lot of lockers, and the receptionist is screaming about Police! And Security! And all the other things that irritated petty authority figures scream about. Can you find the right locker before the courier slips away?

How's your luck holding? Roll one die, and if you're carrying a [Sparkling Icosahedron], add 1.

Roll 3 or more: turn to **78**.

2 or less: you have to give up when you hear the sirens. Turn to **216**.

67

Yes! There are eleven possibilities which have at least one die as 1, and only one of those has the other die as a 1. Great work! Take **+1** {PUZZLER}

You disable the lock, and both cupboards open. Deadpool immediately pushes past you for the right-hand cupboard, and comes out with a glittering lapel badge in the shape of a big grin. "Shiny!" Deadpool says. He starts stroking it.

You may add the [Diamond Smile Pin] to your inventory – max five items, remember – and while you have it with you, you gain **+2 MOUTH**.

The back of the left-hand cupboard door has a rough

map of the complex. You make a note of the route to the command center. There are also three identical lockers in this cupboard, though you have time to open just one of them.

To open locker one, turn to **226**.

To open locker two, turn to **248**.

To open locker three ("This last one has snacks in," Deadpool says, "I can smell 'em!"), turn to **84**.

68

You're squashed in next to Deadpool in the stupid little yellow car, hurtling your way back towards New York City. "I'm glad you're with me, Six. This mission is a stinking heap of organic bovine fertilizer. I used to work for Hammerhead, after they first gave me my healing factor. I'm not proud of it, but I was in a bad place. The point is, he knows the ways my mind doesn't work. I'm going to need you."

"I'll be there," you promise.

"I know." He takes his hands off the wheel to make a cute little heart symbol. "Listen though, Hammerhead is really dangerous. He was a lethally dangerous psychotic back when he was just a Russian pretending to be an Italian to get into the Mafia. Nowadays, he's got an adamantium skeleton, class ten strength, and a whole bunch of other enhancements."

"Class ten?"

"Right, think Spider-Man. Just ridiculously, unnecessarily strong. Utterly pointless. Old H-H has been fighting Kingpin and Dr Octopus for the top New York spot for years now, and I'm sure you know how charming those creeps are. This plan of his is really simple, and simple plans are the best ones. Even if all he does is give Chitauri guns to all the gangs in the country, he'll damage the nation beyond imagination. If he can then pull off his slaughter and take over, he'll be the god-emperor of crime, only without the cool sandworm stuff and the endless clones of Idaho. I can't let that happen."

"I understand." What else can you say?

He sighs heavily. "I can't believe Ma– Daredevil sold me that this was easy. He ought to be a lawyer or something."

A little while later, a thought occurs to you. "Why are we in this car, Deadpool?"

He makes an attempt to perk up. "It's all I can afford. I give so much of my money to orphans and pizza delivery folks that at the end of the calendar month, I–"

You shake your head. "No."

"You're right. I could afford better. I just left it too late. I don't expect much out of life, so when they told me that this was the best that they had, I didn't bothe–"

"No."

"Fine. I'm worried about the planet, OK? It's only got a 200cc engine, so it's really low emission. That's why the top speed is only three mph. Sure, it'll take us a couple of months longer, but that's a small price to pay for keeping Greta happy. I'd do anything for that young–"

"*No!*"

He sighs, suddenly sad again. "You remind me of an old friend. I thought it would be funny, okay?"

"And is it?"

"No. It sucks."

You nod. "Yeah."

If your {CHAOS} is 15 or more, take the ACHIEVEMENT: *You* Have *Been Naughty*.

If your {CHAOS} is 5 or more, or you have {NO (SUB) WAY} or {CENTRAL CRATER} at 1 or – somehow – more, then turn to **44**.

If you don't have any of those things, take the ACHIEVEMENT: *Low Profile*, and turn to **138**.

69

Ooh, you filthy cheat! You know perfectly well that you don't have a [Sledgehammer]. There *is* no [Sledgehammer]. Bet you've got a {KUMQUATS} rating as well. Cheating. At a *gamebook*. We're shocked, reader. Shocked, we tell you.

You know what? Fine. Have it your way. You take your imaginary [Sledgehammer] and use this wild hallucination to hammer through the wall. We hope you're proud.

ACHIEVEMENT: *I Wanna Be Your...*

You go through into a concrete corridor done out in fallout shelter chic. You're at a corner.

To go straight ahead, turn to **221**.

To head left, turn to **273**.

70

Ignoring the surrounding traffic with terrifying disdain, Deadpool calls Weasel on the speakerphone. "Hey, Weas!"

"Hey, Wade. Died recently?"

"Who knows? Is this a Thursday?"

The phone is silent for a moment. "No?"

"No idea, then."

"Sweet."

"We're trying to crack this amazing conspiracy network that Hammerhead has put together."

"Oh, so it's the lug behind it, huh?"

"Yeah."

"So?"

"Can you tell me anything useful?"

"Naturally. Don't stare at the sun, not even in an eclipse. Two wrongs do actually make a right if you do it properly. Crush the garlic clove with the flat of a kitchen knife before peeling it. If the tornado isn't moving, it's heading straight for you. Don't turn your back on a mountain lion. If your house randomly starts smelling like fish, it's probably an electrical fire. How am I doing?"

"Amazing. What about Hammerhead's network?"

Deadpool loosely "explains" about the sites you've discovered and the things you've seen. In return, Weasel comes up with a pile of data that Deadpool seems to make some kind of sense of. The word "traitor" comes up a lot. They gossip on, but do eventually hang up.

Take **+1 {NET OPS}** and **+1 {OUT OF TIME}**. If you are carrying an **[Encrypted File]**, take an extra **+1 {NET OPS}**. If you have **{NO (SUB)WAY}** of 1 or more, take an extra **+1 {OUT OF TIME}** for the congestion.

Now, to research Hammerhead's personnel, turn to **238**.

To get to the safe-house, turn to **216**.

71

You stroll into the shadowy warehouse. No one shouts in protest. All the shelves are empty. Not very promising.

"I was in an invisible warehouse once," Deadpool says.

"How?"

"Carefully. Stubbed my toe anyway. It was agony, you know?"

"Maybe we should be quiet, just in case?"

Deadpool sniffs, but lightens his footsteps and stops talking for a moment. There's a staff room near the back, and you decide to try there.

It's time for a stealth minigame!

Round 1: Roll one die, and add your **FOCUS**. Score 5 or more: you win round 1.

Round 2: Roll one die and add your **FOCUS**. If you won round 1, add **+2**. On an 8 or more, you win round 2.

Did you win Round 2?

Yes: turn to **147**.

No: turn to **131**.

72

Oh, hey. What are *you* doing here? Wait. Where even *is* here?

You're in a blank white void, shining and completely empty. For all you know, you might be plummeting downwards at horrendous speed, unable to tell because of the absence of air to provide resistance. At this speed, maybe you wouldn't even see the ground approaching until you were already dead. It's something to think about as you – yes, really *you*, dear reader – hurtle through the vast, uncaring universe at approximately 650,000 mph, glued to this silly little rock we all share by forces we still don't entirely understand. And people say that *clowns* are scary.

ACHIEVEMENT: *Secret Hunter Six.*

An infinite series of rows of ugly metal shelving appear out of nowhere and engulf you before you have a chance to scream. The shelves are absolutely packed with logs. All the logs in the multiverse. They seem happy and supportive. If you want to grab a [Cheery Log], feel free to take one with you.

Wherever you were before, go back there now.

73

Snow Valley is a beautiful town, quaint white-planked houses with red tiled roofs, well-manicured yards, a historic little shopping district, and a colonial-era town hall.

"They have sensors in the sidewalks," Deadpool says. "If any adult with less than a million dollars is detected, robots are immediately sent to contain the pauper, and dump them outside the town limits."

"Plausible." All *too* plausible, looking at this place.

Your destination is signposted as the Ironbranded, Inc Massachusetts Academy Corporate Retreat and Wellness Center Featuring DiMaggio's Steakhouse and Cocktail Bar. While the name may have metastasized, the Academy itself is still lovely, comprised of several elegant red-bricked structures around a glass-topped central building, all nestled in wooded parkland. The parking lot bristles with expensive sedans and limousines. As you park up, you can feel the cars around you cringing away in horror. A big notice-board at the top of the car-park holds bland welcome posters for the lucky management-tier employees of today's companies, Ad Astra, Mercatech, and Dominion Networks. As you approach the main entrance, you see a professionally smiley young woman in a suit worth more than you want to imagine standing outside. She's carrying a clipboard.

What's your plan?

To pretend to be attendees, turn to **252**.

To look for other ways in, turn to **47**.

To brandish weapons and attack wildly, turn to **20**.

74

The area down the side of the fence smells musky. After a minute or two, you find a ragged hole in the wire, and clamber into the overgrown lot. There are various rusted-out trucks and other pieces of machinery around you. They don't look quite right somehow, but you're distracted by the feeling that someone is watching.

Take **+1 FOCUS**. There's a trampled path of grass here, and a moment later, you discover why as a snarling pack of coyotes advances on the pair of you. Deadpool throws his arms wide and yells at them incoherently.

Make an intimidation test. Roll one die, and add your **MERC** to it. If you score 5 or less, Deadpool gets the back of one leg bitten out in the process of scaring the coyotes off. Take **-1 MERC**.

With the animals gone for now, you look around. There's a large shed that looks like it still holds a few flecks of blue paint, or a boxy storage building with brick walls and a moldering roof.

To try the once-blue shed, go to **32**.

To try the storage building, go to **137**.

75

You're in a strange spot, an intersection with several dark corridors leading off. Lights flicker in the distance, sometimes seeming to progress up the corridor towards you. You find yourself hoping that they don't reach you. There are several doors nearby, each one outlined with dim neon red lights that throb distressingly. Actually, the red ones hold hydrogen rather than neon, but the principle is the same.

After the blandness of the rest of the building so far, it's extremely disorienting. Some sort of security system, perhaps. Deadpool is humming tunelessly and tapping his chin with his fingers.

Make a concentration test. Roll one die and add your **FOCUS**.

Score 8 or more: You shake the effect off.

On a 7 or less: Take **-1 FOCUS**.

Now, peering at the doors, you can make out some labels.

If you want to go into the mapping room, turn to **145**.

If you want to enter the server room, turn to **170**.

If you want to try the boiler room, turn to **116**.

76

You come down into a claustrophobic network of concrete steam tunnels. Guards and office types are bustling back and forth in the dimness, and even the occasional person in overalls. You hear someone call out, but they're already rushing off when you look round. You've definitely been spotted.

Take **+2 {CENTRAL ALERT}**.

Unfortunately, some of the organization's thugs are nearby, and they hear the call as well. A moment later, a half-dozen ripped guys charge towards you.

"Where do they get them all?" Deadpool asks.

This is a simple fight.

Round one: roll two dice and add your **MERC**. If the total is at least 9, you win the first round.

Round two: roll two dice and add your **MERC**. If the total is at least 9, you win the second round.

If you lose both rounds, one of the guards gets an alert off, so take **+1 {CENTRAL ALERT}** and **-1 MERC** because Deadpool is disappointed with himself.

Now, blood-splashed signs on the tunnel walls point towards Administration one way, and Storage the other.

If you want to try Admin, turn to **281**.

If you want to try Storage, turn to **282**.

77

The old warehouse is sagging, but it doesn't collapse when you enter. Which is nice. Inside, there are several pieces of strangely retro-futuristic technology, with dusty ceramic shells and thick bundles of snaking cables and old-fashioned camera aperture ring-shutters. You've no idea what any of it was supposed to do.

"Wow, look at all this junk," Deadpool says cheerfully. "I bet I could make Weasel believe this trash was useful." He picks up a ring-shaped piece of ceramic and alloy painted with soft orange stripes. "I wonder what this is?"

Before you can scream "Nooooooo!" he clicks a hidden switch, and flame gouts out.

Make a luck test. Roll one die. If you roll a 1 or 2, Deadpool's hands get unpleasantly singed. Take **-1 MERC**.

Now, to go over to the red shed you saw, turn to **228**.
To head to the decayed trailer-office out the back, turn
to **168**.

78

"I hear breathing," Deadpool says.

"Well *excuse* me," you grumble. "We just ran a long way.
You're kinda puffed yourself, supermerc."

"Not you. *There.*" He rips a door off its hinge.

Inside, you discover Talon Minor, hunched into a scared
ball. "Please..." the courier begs.

"Give us the list, friendo. I won't let Six murder you, I
promise."

You're playing bad cop? Wow. You try to look like an
enraged psychopath, but you suspect it just comes across
as constipated. Either way, miraculously, it works. Talon
Minor hands over a document.

Take **+1 {NAMES DOWN}**.

"Is that really everything?" Deadpool asks sternly. "It
looks very light for every major criminal in the country."

You bare your teeth and do your best to growl. Aww, bless.

Make a very easy persuasion test. Roll one die and add
your **MOUTH**.

On a score of 5 or more: Talon Minor shudders, and hands over a wad more paperwork. Take +2 {NAMES DOWN}.

On 4 or less: Talon Minor insists that is all, and the approaching sirens drive you off. Take -1 MOUTH.

You head back to the safe-house, while Deadpool takes photos of the list, and emails them to Weasel for distribution. Turn to **216**.

79

As you all watch, the black helicopter shimmers and disappears into the background. "Yeah, no way I can follow that," the pilot says. "I'm sure I've seen similar machines taking off from this warehouse complex over the last few days though. I'll take you there."

Deadpool's been complaining about modern nautical pirate standards for ten minutes straight, when the pilot points out a warehouse complex ahead, complete with helipad and multiple yards. "This is where I've seen them."

As you approach, you notice that there are a lot of men with machine-guns pointing up towards you. "Maybe we should back off," you suggest.

"Aww," Deadpool says. "You could just drop me in there. It'll be fun."

"Not yet," you say. "See that?" From the air, you can clearly see a large stack of crates deep in one of the complex's yard spaces. They're covered by a tarp that has the name SECOND FAMILY stenciled onto it.

"They've started shooting!" The pilot immediately takes the copter up and away. "Get what you need?"

"It's a lead," you say.

Take **+1 {SUSPICIOUS NAME}** and the ACHIEVEMENT: *Flying High.*

To follow up on your lead, turn to **86**.

Or, if you haven't already:

To try underground routes, turn to **179**.

To try surface routes, turn to **43**.

80

You cross the corridor to Professor Hope's office and knock.

"Enter," says an impatient, plummy voice.

Deadpool pushes the door open and strides in.

"Oh, look, a fool and his puppy." The professor is in his late fifties, sleek and well-groomed, with the face of a jaded Victorian esthete run to seed. He waves you away disgustedly. "Go back to Mirocaw or Carcosa or whatever you think you're doing, and let me work."

Deadpool walks up to the big, plush oak desk, and leans on it. "My name is Deadpool. We need to ask–"

"I don't care." The professor sits up a little straighter, and flips a switch in one arm of his desk chair. A claxon sounds momentarily, the door slams shut, and the professor – and his chair – vanish back into a gaping hole where a bookcase had been a moment before. Then everything lurches, and the section of floor you're on plummets down into the ground.

When it crunches to a stop, you're in a metal-walled room with one heavy-looking steel security door.

To use your [Sledgehammer], turn to **69**.

To crawl through an air vent, turn to **234**.

To smash through the door, turn to **296**.

81

There are eleven possibilities where at least one die is a 1. Only one of those possibilities has the other die as a 1. So it's 1 in 11. Sorry.

"Great work, Mariachi," Deadpool says.

You only partially disable the lock. The left-hand cupboard opens a little, showing you a rough map of the complex. You make a note of the route to the command center. There are also three identical lockers in this cupboard, but you have time to open just one of them.

To open locker one, turn to **226**.

To open locker two, turn to **248**.

To open locker three, turn to **84**.

You peek inside nervously. The security room is absolutely chaotic. Red warning lights are flashing, a huge bank of monitors shows an ever-evolving set of scenes with suited people running this way and that, and numerous computer terminals are blinking urgent messages. There's a dozen people in here, most shouting into cellphones or radio handsets, and they all seem to be dashing between desks, terminals, filing cabinets, and the such. They do not immediately notice you.

If you have a [Security Pass], you can access a terminal near the door to dismiss a couple of alarms, and take -2 {WARNED}.

There are some yellow lab coats over the back of a chair nearby. If you'd like [Disguises], take them.

Now you need to leave, but the monitors can show you how busy the next floor is going to be.

If you want to go up in a calm moment, turn to **139**.

If you want to meet some more guards, turn to **132**.

83

You climb down the ladder into the middle of a circular white room. Three curved metal doors are set into the wall, spaced evenly. As you come down, there's a faint grinding and the wall begins to spin, faster and faster, the doors blurring into invisibility. Then it slams to a stop with an audible *thunk*.

It's time for a progress minigame!

Make a luck test. Roll one die. If you're carrying a [Walkie-Talkie], subtract 1 because the background guard chatter helps. If you get 4 or less: a door opens onto a corridor. Turn immediately to **24**.

Otherwise, a door opens to admit a small group of guards, leading to a simple but nasty little fight.

Round one: roll two dice and add your **MERC**. If your total is at least 9, you win the first round.

Round two: roll two dice and add your **MERC**. If the total is at least 9, you win the second round.

If your {DRAGONFIRE} is less than 3 and you lost at least one round, take -1 MERC.

If your {DRAGONFIRE} is 3 or more and you lost at least one round, take -1 MERC for each round you lost.

Now, take +1 {DRAGONFIRE}. The rotating wall starts up again.

If your {DRAGONFIRE} is 4 or more, turn to entry **219**.

Otherwise, restart this entry from the beginning. Darn!

84

You open the third locker. You can already hear boots approaching faintly. Inside is a handful of [Candies]. Mmm, candies. They're heart-shaped, so they must be good for you. You can eat the candies now for +1 MERC, or take them to eat later. Once you eat them, they're gone. Life is tragedy, when you get right down to it. Now you need to get moving before someone actually sane and threatening finds you.

To head to the command suite, turn to **232**.

To head to the storage area, turn to **282**.

85

You follow Deadpool to the lobby door. "Better wait here, Sixy. It's going to get a bit special in there." He bursts in, guns ready. The blue-suited guards seem surprised, but they open fire.

This is a hard fight.

Round one: roll two dice and add your **MERC** and your {CASH DOWN} – the thing about hirelings is that they do expect to be paid. If the total is at least 13, you win the first round.

Round two: roll two dice and add your **MERC** and your {CASH DOWN}. If the total is at least 13, you win the second round.

Round three: roll three dice and add your **MERC** and your {CASH DOWN}. If the total is at least 15, you win the third round.

Eventually Deadpool is the only one standing, and it's reasonably safe to go in. It looks like it went reasonably well, provided you were a mercenary in a garish red outfit with some fascinating personality disorders.

If you lost any rounds, take **-1 MERC**.

As you pick your way through, you see many of the corpses wearing a **[Security Pass]**. You may take one, assuming you have space in your inventory.

Now, if you want to use the elevators onwards, turn to **249**.

If you would rather take the stairs, turn to **171**.

86

At a table in a shabby little deli, Deadpool phones a friend while you eat an unremarkable bagel.

"It's me," he says. "Who do you think? Well sure, I could be, if she had a throat injury and had lost her freaking mind. That is *never* going to happen. What? No. Ugh. Even Fabian couldn't pull that off. She has lawyers. No, never mind. I'm in… Sixmeister, where are we?"

"New York?" you suggest.

He nods and speaks into the phone again. "I'm in New York. Wrong again, amigo. What can you tell me about a group called Second Family? Could be hackers, could be lawyers, could be Greek shipping magnates. No, of course I have a clue, I just told you. Sheesh, don't you ever listen? Yes, I've got a pen… Six, remember this. A red warehouse on Clintonville Street, and a bar on Morningside called The Hollow. Got it. Later." He hangs up. "You did get that, right?"

You nod.

"So where we headed?"

"The bar." Turn to **240**.

"The warehouse." Turn to **126**.

87

There's a bunch of rumors out there about the assassinations. There always is on a covert op – spooks call it "footprint" and it's functionally unavoidable. Putting the shreds together is significantly tricky, however.

This is a puzzle to mimic the challenge of you trying to locate the list's courier.

Below, you'll find five heroes. Four of them have been associated with the X-Men. One has not – but who?

If you think Abyss is the odd one out, turn to **59**.

Darwin? Turn to **107**.

Forearm? Turn to **61**.

Lifeguard? Turn to **37**.

Warbird? Turn to **212**.

88

Deadpool is covered in ghastly fluids, and he's limping a bit, but the lesser monstrosities lie broken, starting to dissolve. The huge flesh-colored horror extends its spidery limbs out even further than you feared, and advances. Its cautious approach and probing feints reveal a canny intelligence. This thing can *think*.

"Mwah." Deadpool blows it a kiss.

This is phase two of a boss fight.

The horror fights defensively, parrying blows with its razor-sharp claws and keeping Deadpool at range.

Round 1: roll two dice and add your **FOCUS** twice. If the total is at least 14, you win the first round.

Round 2: roll two dice and add your **MOUTH** and **MERC**. If the total is at least 15, you win the second round.

Round 3: roll two dice and add your **MERC** and your {**CHAOS**}. Sanity is not always the correct response. If the total is at least 15, you win the third round.

Round 4: roll one die, and add the number of wins you got in rounds 1 to 3. Sometimes, it all comes down to luck. If the total is 5 or more, you win the fourth round.

If you won that 4th round, turn to **112**.

If you lost, turn to **17**.

89

The dragon wing is a bit more ostentatious than the flower wing. Gold and red dominate, the floor is cut to look like rush mats, and pictures of long, sinuous dragons leer from the stretches of wall between doors. Deadpool tuts and shakes his head. You've not got far at all when a couple of suit-wearing guards appear.

"I'm afraid you'll have to go back to the flower wing," one of them says. He's perfectly polite, but still menacing.

"Or?" asks Deadpool, seemingly pleasantly.

"There is no 'or.'"

"Oh, there is always an 'or.' Always."

The guy scowls. "Not this time."

If you want to start a fight, turn to **13**.

If you want to try the pond corridor, turn to **92**.

90

After the rest of this area, the bathroom is a nasty shock. It's dingy and claustrophobic, with cracked mirrors and stained metal sinks. The small light flickers nastily, as if the bulb is about to give out. There is a stall, but it's hidden in a deep well of shadow. Is there such a thing as a punishment toilet?

Undeterred, Deadpool looks towards the stall. "If we've got a couple of minutes..."

If you choose to indulge him, wait outside and take **+1 MOUTH**, but also **+1 {CENTRAL ALERT}**.

To check the breakfast nook, turn to **294**.

To go meet the boss, turn to **191**.

91

"No one ever thinks to look up," you point out.

Deadpool immediately looks up, scraping his forehead on the car's low roof. "I can see why. This is dumb." He starts the car and shoots out into the road, his face still jammed against the roof.

"Road!" you yelp. He looks down again, swerving around a post truck that's busy crashing into some parked cars in an effort to avoid flattening you. "I meant, maybe the smugglers are using the air," you say.

"Nice. Yes, I know just the guy."

Fifteen minutes later, you're parked in the lot of HeliCity Wonder Sky Tours, grateful to have made it through the city alive. Deadpool pops out of the tiny rental like a cork out of a bottle. You unfold yourself and follow him, ignoring a twinge in your spine.

As he crosses the lot, you distinctly see a man in a garish flight suit duck behind a large tub of flowers. Unfortunately for him, Deadpool sees him too and bounces over, jumping onto the flowers to look down at him. "Bob!"

The man straightens back up. His flight suit has the name ROBERT DAVIES stitched over the breast. "Hello, Mr Wilson." His voice is deeply reluctant.

"I need you, Bob. Right here, right now. The fate of the free world is at stake!"

The man sighs. "Look, I'm waiting for a group of Japanese executives. They'll be here any minute. It's a two-hour tour. Maybe after—"

Deadpool turns back to you and whispers, far too loudly, "We can't just *kill* him. Or can you fly a helicopter?"

Robert gives you the saddest, most plaintive look you've ever seen on any creature that wasn't a lonely puppy.

If you want to try coercion, turn to **181**.

If you'd like to see if you can join the tour, turn to **251**.

If you rather give truth a chance, turn to **142**.

92

You find yourself in an odd corridor. The walls are painted in muddy blues and greens, the ceiling is a lighter blue, and the floor is deep teal. Water weed, rocks and koi carp are painted on the walls and floor as if at a distance. It's nasty. Towards the end, a door is half-open. It leads to a sterile white antechamber with a metal ladder that plunges downward.

"I had a nightmare like this once. I was tortured for days. Wait, no, that really happened. Anyway, what I'm saying is fish belong in tacos."

Make a security test. Roll one die, and add your {DRAGONFIRE}, if any.

If the total is 6 or more: turn to **129**.

4 or 5: turn to **208**.

1 to 3: turn to **83**.

93

You lose sight of the truck for a moment, but you catch it as it heads onto the freeway.

"Grab the wheel," Deadpool says.

Suddenly he's climbing onto you and shoving you over. The little car veers wildly, and horns blare at you, but somehow you keep from crashing. The car has almost stopped by the time you're wedged in enough to control it, but you gamely set off after the truck.

"Bring me alongside," Deadpool says. "A long side. That's a silly word. You can totally be alongside a short side, but I'd never say 'bring me ashortside.' That would just be embarrassing."

He keeps on, but you're driving. The truck has slowed to avoid suspicion, and as you're crossing a bridge, you get near the truck driver's door. Deadpool squeezes out and jumps onto the truck. His sword flashes, and the truck's tire explodes. It careens wildly towards the bridge railing, then plummets down into the river. You watch it fall in horror, then realize Deadpool is clinging to the railing, dangling the driver over the river. Everything screeches to a halt.

The truck driver is shrieking. Below him, hundreds of high-end suit bags are floating up to the surface of the river. "Help!" the driver screams. "Hijackers! Help! Police! Oh God, help!"

Oops. Wrong truck. Take **+1 {CHAOS}** and the ACHIEVEMENT: *$100k Penguin Suit Ruin*.

If you have {SUSPICIOUS NAME} of 1 or more and want to use that lead, turn to entry **86**.

Or instead, if you haven't already:

To try underground routes, by turning to **179**.

To try air routes, turn to **91**.

94

You pull Deadpool aside. "It might be a trap. I mean, he says he's a fan but…"

Deadpool frowns, but then shrugs. "Tell you what," he says to Todd. "I'll do it myself."

As dozens of students crowd round to film everything, Deadpool pulls out a sword with his right hand and slowly pushes it through his left palm, up to the hilt. He stifles a groan and bows for the collected gasps, then pulls the sword back out and sheathes it. The hole in his hand seals back over almost immediately. The crowd cheers and applauds.

"This is such an amazing day," Todd babbles. "You've made me so happy."

"Do you know where we can find Professor Hope?" you put in.

Todd looks crestfallen. "I'm sorry, it's a big faculty. Try the administration block or the library? I can direct you to either."

If you want to try admin, turn to **161**.

If you want to try the library, turn to **299**.

95

You gesture to the door. "Let's do this."

"Now you're talking sense," Deadpool says.

"That's worrying."

"Isn't it though?" He pulls out his guns, and marches through the doors of the Meteorite Building and into the lobby. You hang back and watch as the blue-suited guards pull up their machine-guns and open fire. Huh. Good soundproofing. Take **+1** {WARNED}.

This is a hard fight.

Round one: roll two dice and add your **MERC** and your {CASH DOWN} – hirelings do expect payment. If the total is at least 15, you win the first round.

Round two: roll two dice and add your **MERC** and your {CASH DOWN}. If the total is at least 15, you win the second round.

Round three: roll three dice and add your **MERC** and your {CASH DOWN}. If the total is at least 18, you win the third round.

Eventually, Deadpool is the only one standing, and it's reasonably safe to go in, so you can discover how much punishment he took.

If you won every round, take **-1 MERC**.

If you lost any rounds, take **-2 MERC**.

As you pick your way over the blue slaughter, you notice that many of the guards are wearing a [Security Pass]. You can take one with you, if you want – five items maximum though, remember.

Now, if you want to use the elevators, turn to **249**.
If you would rather take the stairs, turn to **171**.

96

It's easy to get a surreptitious look at the ship. It's definitely seen better days, but it's much like the various other ships you've seen around the docks. Which makes sense, really. What sets it apart is the presence of several bald, bull-necked thugs in black roll-necked sweaters openly carrying machine-guns. You watch for a few minutes, and see that there is a steady stream of equally muscular workers bringing crates down to the ship, getting instructions, and then carrying the crates to one of several trucks kept under equally heavy guard. One of the trucks is close to full. If you go get the car, you can try following it, or you can send Deadpool in to attack.

To try following the truck, turn to **207**.
To attack the thugs, turn to **21**.

97

Deadpool hears you, and deftly removes the piece you identified. The tower lurches, but doesn't quite fall. Jengarm nods resignedly and does his best, but the instant he touches the stack, it all collapses into a bouncing heap of gore. He shakes his head once, then beams in delight. "Is first time I lose in six years. Wonderful! You truly are magnificent. So. We have deal. I tell you where to find controller."

"Wait… controller?" Deadpool says. "You're not the boss?"

"Me?" He laughs, sincerely amused. "No. I keep art and turn fools into money. But boss of whole country I do not even know name of. Is very big plan, yes? Very clever. But controller of my northeast network part, I know. Professor of Folklore at college named Coreham, near Boston. Ivy league. Very fancy. His name is Hope. Mudak. He knows where to find boss, or so he boasts."

"Thank you, Aleksandr," Deadpool says. "I need a month-long shower, but it's been a pleasure."

"I agree. It has. One day, we play again, yes? If is possible, I help you later."

Set {UNLIKELY ALLY} to 1 and add the ACHIEVEMENT: *I'm a Machine.*

You don't get to shower, but you do clean up, and the Russian has some clever gel-sticks that pull the blood out of your clothing. With many hearty and cheerful goodbyes ringing in your ears, you set out for Boston.

To scout out Coreham College, turn to **287**.

To just go straight there, turn to **148**.

The mayhem dies down, and you do not appear to be injured. You look up from behind the jukebox. The bar is littered with bodies, and there is blood everywhere. The serving area is on fire, and even as you look, a bottle of spirits shatters in a blast of flame and glass. Deadpool is on the floor, one arm sporting an exciting new compound fracture, but he has his legs wrapped around the neck of a particularly big, unhappy-looking thug. Behind them, your eyes drift over a poster that reads "Straczinsky A1B2C3 – America's Best Big Classy Cider Cup." The gore splattering it detracts from the effect.

Take **+1 {CHAOS}** and **-1 MERC**.

"I can snap your neck," Deadpool is saying to the henchman. "Or you can tell me about Second Family. Or both." He twists a bit.

The thug shrieks. "No!" The smoke is getting thicker. You don't fancy the building's chances.

"No to which?"

"You want One Family, Inc. Second is one of our, uh, *their* divisions. There's a place in Bethesda Terrace Arcade in Central Park. You said you wouldn't kill me."

Deadpool lets the guy go, and then tugs on his own shattered arm, wincing as the bone shards slide back in. While the guy tries to catch his breath, and various other wounded try to crawl for the door, Deadpool leads you outside. You can hear sirens converging from every direction. "Let's get going," he says.

To research One Family, Inc, turn to **175**.

To head straight over to Central Park, turn to **48**.

99

"I was hoping for something a bit more interesting," Deadpool says. "But I trust you." He walks up to the guards, says "Hey, fellas," and then slugs one right in the mouth.

This is a very simple fight.

Round one: roll two dice and add your **MERC**. If the total is at least 7, you win too quickly for either guard to call for backup. If you lose, take **+1 {ROLLING STONE}**.

Then Deadpool grabs a security card and swipes it, and the door makes a clicking sound. There's a big red button next to the door as well though.

If you tug on the door, turn to **160**.

If you push the button, turn to **55**.

100

The pilot brings you in closer to the news copter. It seems curious, and as you approach, Deadpool leans forward.

"That's Trish Hutchins from New York News Now!" He starts waving frantically. Oh great. It really is a news copter. As the news crew swing round to point their camera in your direction, Deadpool throws open the door of the helicopter and swings round to sit facing them.

"Are they live?" you ask the pilot.

A moment later, you hear a crackle in your headset and then a woman is talking in a professionally excited news voice. "...here in the sky live with the hero Deadpool! Maybe he'll give us an interview, folks."

Deadpool is frantically making "call me" gestures, and waving his phone at the camera. If you really want to allow Deadpool to give an interview, turn to **275**.

If not, you need a distraction – you think for a moment. "Hey," you say. "I just saw Ryan Reynolds get into that car!" You point at a random car passing underneath. Deadpool immediately orders the pilot to swoop down and follow. Your helicopter chases a really freaked-out businessman's car for five minutes before you tell Deadpool you were wrong. Although he's unhappy, the news copter has left.

Take +1 {DISCORD}.

The only thing left to do is head after the black helicopter. Turn to **29**.

101

Despite your combined best efforts, the black helicopter seems to have just vanished. Maybe it landed somewhere out of sight. Either way, you can't find it. After forty-five minutes of fruitless further searching, Deadpool gets bored. When you talk him out of just jumping out of the copter, he demands to be taken back to the helipad. The pilot is only too happy to oblige.

ACHIEVEMENT: *The Blinded Eye*.

If you have {SUSPICIOUS NAME} of 1 and want to use that lead, turn to **86**.

Or, if you haven't already:

Try underground routes by turning to **179**.

To try surface routes, turn to **43**.

102

There is a surprising number of small, quietly private banks spread across New York. They have restricted customer bases, and sit out of the way of most foot traffic. The pair of you park up near one which seems to be linked to Hammerhead's network. It's an attractive building that fits nicely with the quiet, leafy street, but not so much with the extensive amount of noisy road construction happening at the other end of the road.

Deadpool is staring back at the roadworks. "We could walk in guns blazing, but you know, I've always wanted an earthmover. Oh, don't look like that. These people are criminals. They don't call cops, just their own enforcers. There's nothing to worry about."

To raid the bank the old-fashioned way, turn to **105**.

To smash a wall down, turn to **155**.

103

"Okay, let's try a trick," you say.

You can feel Deadpool beaming at you through his mask. "Right." He takes a big painting of a forest lake off the wall, and wrestles it over to the door. Then he starts hammering on the wood, and yells, "Open up! He's coming! He's coming! The boss said we've got to save this... Pollock? Quick!"

Can you fast-talk your way out of this? Roll one die, and add your **MOUTH** to what you get. If you get 6 or less, turn to **186** now.

If not… the door cracks open, and a deeply suspicious face peers out. Deadpool is already striking with the butt of his gun, and the guard doesn't even have time to blink before he's toppling back, eyes glazed.

"Sucker." Deadpool pushes the door wider. As it opens, you can see that it's actually a vault door set in reinforced concrete, just paneled over with a cheap wood laminate. Inside is a small room with a number of enigmatic, code-filled terminal displays which opens onto a short, blandly gray corridor. There are doors to the left and the right.

To try the left door, turn to **222**.

To try the right door, turn to **27**.

104

You go through into the kitchen, a gleaming place of chrome and steel, with a huge dumb-waiter set in one wall. The whole place is filled with all manner of potential weapons – knives, pans, three pots of boiling stuff, several fridges that could certainly crush someone, a dozen pairs of sharp-looking chopsticks, a melon baller... The list goes on. Wow – kitchens are *deadly*. There's a guy in a chef's outfit staring at you both in horror, groping for an intercom in the wall.

"Oh, hi," Deadpool says pleasantly. The cook blanches.

Can you stop him from raising the alarm?

If you have {DARK SECRET} of 1 or more, you find that you know exactly how to drive him into catatonia with your maddening whispers. You eldritch abomination, you.

If you give him a [Rubber Chicken], he's so completely bewildered and offended that he wanders off and hides in the fridge.

Otherwise, you'll have to try to persuade him. Roll one die and add your MOUTH.

8 or more: He does back away before fleeing.

7 or less: He presses the button, and then backs away and flees anyway. Take +1 {CHEF!}

> Now, before anything else happens, if you want to investigate the dumb-waiter, turn to **189**.
>
> If you want to go to the corridor nearby, turn to **149**.

105

"Assassins" sounds bad, but you've definitely been identified by the network by now. Worse? How could it possibly be worse? You walk in, Deadpool with his pistols drawn.

"Vault!" he bellows.

Everyone screams, people dive for cover, alarms go off, and havoc ensues. However, you both clearly see the nearest teller's eyes flick involuntarily off to the right. You go that way, ignoring the hubbub. The huge vault door is built into the wall, and it hasn't closed yet, but there's a group of very well-armed paramilitary guards outside it. They see you, and start shooting.

This is a moderate fight.

Round one: roll two dice and add your **MERC**. If the total is at least 12, you win the first round.

Round two: roll two dice and add your **MERC**. If the total is at least 11, you win the second round.

Round three: roll two dice and add your **MERC**. If the total is at least 10, you win the third round.

> If you win two or more rounds, you drive off the mercs. Turn to **177**.
>
> If you lose two or more rounds, you are forced to retreat. Turn to **216**.

106

With the plan disrupted and Hammerhead thrown in Super-Supermax, the plan fizzles. There are still some alien guns out there, but not enough for any sort of critical mass, and the wave of gang violence never happens.

Life gets back to normal after that, so you're surprised to get home one evening to find a suitcase rammed full of money and note from Deadpool that says: *"Your share of the take, Number One. Next time? XoxoX."*

ACHIEVEMENT: *Crushing Victory*.

If you have an **[Artisanal Stick Candy]**, now is the time to munch it, and take the extra ACHIEVEMENT: *Lolly*.

Final score: 3 stars.

The end.

107

Darwin, whose real name is Armando Muñoz, has been a member of X-Men teams on a number of occasions, saving Professor X more than once. He is not the odd one out. Sorry. Go back to **216**.

To your relief, Deadpool and the big man are both on solid ground now, squaring off. Deadpool has a gun and a sword out, while the boss has his gorgeous suit, ugly prehensile feet, and a sneer that implies he eats swords and bullets for breakfast. Which might be true. Who knows? Not you.

This is a boss fight.

First, calculate your {PENALTY} by looking at your {DRAGONFIRE}:

Rating of -1 or worse:	0
5-7:	2
2-4:	1
8+:	3

If your {MOOKIGNORE} is 1, add 1 more to your {PENALTY}, for a total of 0-4 depending on how badly it's all gone so far.

Now for round one: roll three dice, subtract your {PENALTY}, then add your MERC and your MOUTH. If the total is at least 13, you win the first round.

Round two: roll three dice, subtract your {PENALTY}, and add double your MERC. If the total is at least 12, you win the second round.

Round three: roll two dice and add your MERC – no penalty this time. If the total is at least 10, you win the third round.

If won two or more rounds, turn to **300**.

If you lost two or more rounds, turn to **197**.

109

There's a lull in the fighting. A whole bunch of the guards are down – fifteen, at a quick count. Despite this, you get the feeling that they're not so much trying to kill Deadpool as to take him down long enough to capture him. That's worrying, as is the way the guards appear to be preparing something.

Take **+1 {ROLLING STONE}**.

A weighted nets flies out from behind the guards towards Deadpool. Help him evade it by rolling one die, and add your **FOCUS** to it.

Score 7 or more: You shout a warning in time. Turn to **247**.

6 or less: Before you can shout, something cracks your head, and it all goes black. Turn to **33**.

110

The flickering firelight leads you to the heart of this accursed place, a perfectly spherical chamber digested out of the rock. It's murder on the ankles. Burning torches spike out in a ring about a third of the way up, dancing in the draft. Within this ring is a scene straight out of a nightmare. A pack of grotesque monstrosities cavort silently on the curving floor. They are part alien machinery, part rotting fungal overgrowth, part tentacle-laden slime – but these things were human once. There are still agonized heads on some, and recognizable limbs on others. This court of madness is presided over by a towering impossibility: a spindly, flesh-colored mantis-like thing with wicked claws, paper-thin wings, and a head that looks like a ball of thin spikes.

"I wonder if they're single," Deadpool says. "Hey, gorgeous, you single?"

The horror buzzes loathsomely, the seething noise almost seeming to form the word *KILLLL*. The tide of atrocity surges towards you.

This is phase one of a boss fight. Deadpool takes one look at his pistols, then draws his katanas and bounces into the fray. Only massive damage seems to slow these things down.

Round 1: roll two dice and add your **MOUTH** and **MERC**. If the total is at least 15, you win the first round.

Round 2: roll two dice and add your **MOUTH** and **MERC**. If the total is at least 16, you win the second round.

If you won at least one round, turn to **88**.

If you lost both rounds, turn to **17**.

111

We're thoroughly programmed to be a little crazy about gold. You stand there for a minute or more, surrounded by gold bars, just staring. It's so beautiful. So shiny. Forbidden butter.

Deadpool snaps out of it first, and piles a cart full of bullion. Wow, he really *is* strong. It's not until you get out onto the street that you start wondering what you're supposed to do with it all. Then, of course, the construction workers notice you, and so do a bunch of pedestrians, and people driving past, and even tellers from the bank, and it turns out we're actually thoroughly programmed to be a *lot* crazy about gold.

Take **+2 {CASH DOWN}**.

Then make an intimidation test. Roll one die, and add your **MERC**.

Score of 7 or more: You load up with gold and drive off, leaving the rest behind. Take **+1 {FLUSH}** and **+1 {CHAOS}**.

6 or less: You're mobbed. Take **+2 {CHAOS}**.

Now head back to the safe-house at **216**.

112

With a hideous high-pitched buzzing whine, the horror collapses, dissolving to pink slime. In the wall, a door opens.

"The good ones are always taken," Deadpool manages, but his heart isn't in it.

You exit, and find yourself on a short platform that opens onto a deep pit. There's another platform forty feet away, with a metal door, and something metallic set into the edge facing you.

"A sliding walkway," Deadpool says. "Cute! I haven't seen one of those for ages. And that looks like a facial recognition scanner." He thinks about it for a moment. "I can't throw you that far, Six. Sorry. Wait, I know." He vanishes back, then returns a minute later cradling four human heads, each caught in expressions of sheer agony. "Come on. We've got four tries."

This is a minigame of head toss!

Roll two dice, and add your **MERC** and **FOCUS**.

If the total is 19 or more, turn to **15**. If not, try again, to a maximum of four attempts.

If you fail every time, turn to **2**.

113

"Maybe we can take out some of those weapons caches. That's got to be useful."

"Roadtrip! I'll steal a bigger car."

"Or we could call in some help?"

Deadpool sighs. "That's no fun. But sure, you're the sane one."

You feel yourself doubting that assessment, but let it go. You've seen a lot of maps regarding this conspiracy, but does Deadpool have good-enough connections to firmly locate at least some of the weapons dumps?

Take **+1 {OUT OF TIME}**.

Make a networking test: roll one die, and add your **MOUTH**, and if you have any, your {NET OPS} and your {NAMES DOWN}.

Score of 7 or more: You get a pile of complex data. Go to **192**.

6 or less: No one is talking. Go back to **216**.

Against all the odds, the duelists have managed to remove maybe a fifth of the limb segments from the disgusting tower. It's starting to sway quite dramatically now, and the stench is dizzying. You're starting to think you might like to give up food entirely, and survive purely on liquids from now on.

"You *is* good," Jengarm booms, casually slipping an elbow segment out from under an ankle. "I knew it! Is very rare to find good player. Is very happy day."

"I worked in Japan for several years," Deadpool replies modestly. He twitches a chunk of calf out from down near the base.

The tower is going to fall any moment now. Both men know it, and Jengarm snatches a piece carefully but quickly, passing the buck. From your position a few feet back, you can see a segment that might buy Deadpool a crucial second.

Make a horrifying game test!

Roll three dice and add your **MERC**, your **FOCUS**, and your **{PUZZLER}** attribute, if any, as you attempt to quickly get Deadpool to take the right piece. If you score 19 or more, he hears you and takes your advice.

Did you win?

If yes, go to **97**.

If no, go to **259**.

115

"We really ought to at least reveal the hit-list, and ideally warn the targets," you argue.

"Protect the worst scum in the country? That's quite the moral complexity, Double-Three. Good causes, slippery slopes, best intentions... Let's go for a slide." First, of course, you need to find the list.

Take **+1 {OUT OF TIME}**.

Make a connections test: Roll one die, and add your **MERC**, and if you have any, your **{ORG SEC}** and your **{WEAPONS DOWN}**.

> Score of 7 or more: You've got some hints about a courier. Go to **87**.
>
> 6 or less: No luck. Go back to **216**.

116

The boiler room is crawling with heavy pipes that enter the walls at seemingly arbitrary locations and odd angles. The space is poorly lit and it's difficult to see much in here, but the furnace that dominates everything does shed some light. It's big and old-fashioned, with very large, soot-stained metal doors and viewing ports. Two of the three view ports are lit right now. Past it, there's another door, so that the boiler room serves as a connection between Research and Data.

The dark viewing port, "+C", has a note scratched in the soot. It reads, *Ego uror supervacuis.*

"I burn away that which is unneeded," Deadpool says.

You blink at him. "Really?"

"Yep."

"I didn't know you spoke Latin."

"Is that what it is?"

"Yes."

"Cool," he says.

If you want to go to the disorienting intersection in Data, turn to **75**.

If you want to go to the science labs in Research, turn to **295**.

117

Using your cell phone for light, you pick your way along the tunnel in front of you. After a disorientingly wild minute or so, the tunnel stops. There's a small table with a note and a plate. The note describes the author's existential despair, at some length. The plate holds a glass of [Milk] you can take. Yeah, sure. "Milk." Let's go with that.

To return to the junction and go left, turn to **276**.

To return to the junction and go right, turn to **31**.

118

The glow leads you into a clearly artificial chamber, cut from the rock so precisely as to leave the walls looking polished. Several metal benches have been set up in here, and they are bristling with clean, functional equipment. It shares something of its design with the old debris you saw above ground, but none of it is precisely identifiable. Some bits buzz, others glow, or hum, or flash intricate color patterns.

"Hey!" You look round to where Deadpool is examining a shining green cylinder. "There's a brain in here!"

You hurry over. He's right, it *is* a brain. "Ugh."

"Hey, don't be so judgmental. You'll hurt its feelings." He reaches down and flicks a switch.

"*Greetings.*" The voice coming from the cylinder is horrible, emotionless and metallic. "*Do not be alarmed. I have many things to tell you.*"

Make a sanity check. Roll one die, and add your **FOCUS** to it.

On an 8 or more: Your mind refuses to process the words. Time passes, that is all.

7 or less: You listen, horrified, as your world reels. Take **-1 MOUTH**, **-1 FOCUS**, and **+1 {DARK SECRET}**. Eventually, worryingly satisfied, the brain allows you both to stagger off.

Further on, the green glow gives way to firelight, but that draft is still at your back.

To follow the firelight, turn to **110**.

To follow the draft, turn to **127**.

119

"We need to make sure we're properly prepared for this," you say.

Deadpool nods. "You can never have too many toys. I'll make some calls."

Take +1 {OUT OF TIME}

Now make a networking test: Roll one die, and add your **MOUTH**, and if you have any, your {NET OPS}, your {FLUSH}, and your {CASH DOWN}.

> On a score of 7 or more: You have some options. Go to **223**.
>
> 6 or less: No one is picking up. Go back to **216**.

120

You try the glassy route. It looks laser-cut. "Only the smoothest routes for Number Six, I see," Deadpool says. "There's nothing quite like silky softness, is there? The gentle caress of a spring breeze, velvet pillows surrounding you–" It's almost a relief when the floor vanishes soundlessly beneath you, and you drop uncomfortably into a sheer pit, about ten feet deep.

Make a climbing test. Roll one die, and add your **MERC** to it.

On a 7 or more: You manage to clamber out easily enough.

5-6: It's slow, but working together, you escape. Take +1 {STUCK FOR A TIME}.

4 or less: It seems to take forever to get out. Take +1 {STUCK FOR A TIME} and -2 MOUTH.

On the other side is a junction. The glow leads onwards, but there's a strong draft blowing from another passage.

To follow the glow, turn to **118**.

To follow the draft, turn to **127**.

121

Deadpool leaps up and down on the locker like an enraged Sentinel, shrieking at it. It resists for a moment, then crumples, and you hear something break. The door pops open with a sad ping. Whatever was in there has been destroyed.

You hear a hiss, and look up. Uh-oh. Gas? You try to hold your breath, but the world goes fuzzy, and you slump to the ground…

Turn to **33**.

122

You sneak round the back of the warehouse, and Deadpool stops. A half-dozen well-built henchmen are gathered back there – it looks like they're gathered around a tablet PC watching a TikTok – and they've all turned to stare.

"Hi!" Deadpool says. "My name is Ted, and I'm here to clean the pool."

Tedpool?

They start pulling guns out – can you blame them? Deadpool rolls forward to take cover behind a large metal trash bin. You duck behind the warehouse.

This is a simple fight.

Round one: roll two dice and add your **MERC**. If the total is at least 8, you win the first round.

Round two: roll two dice and add your **MERC**. If the total is at least 7, you win the second round.

If you win at least one round, the thugs are routed, and you can head into the warehouse. Turn to **147**.

If you lost both rounds, you decide to retreat and try the bar instead. Turn to **240**.

123

"Nice," Deadpool says, grabbing a marker and scribbling an address label. "Remind me to let Weasel know what to do with these before he just sells them, or goes on a murderous rampage, or decides to excavate the whole of Fifth Avenue, again."

Take **+1 {NOBBLED GUNS}** and **+2 {TERRIFYING WEASEL}**.

Nothing bad will come of sending a half-dozen crates of hellish alien weaponry to Deadpool's best friend. Oh no. Nothing bad at all.

If you go on to the command suite, turn to entry **232**.

If you stay in Shipping, turn to **255**, but don't come back here. Really, please don't.

124

You go through the security door into a stretch of corridor that takes you to the foot of a flight of stairs. You head on up into a large area that looks a bit like the changing room at a gym, minus the showers.

"I wish I knew where my towel was," Deadpool says. "It ran away screaming weeks ago, though. I think it's in the Caribbean now."

"I don't blame it," you mutter.

He slugs you gently on the shoulder. "That's the spirit!"

There are several simple lockers in here, most of them open and empty, but there's also a much larger, fancier one standing free at the end of a row of benches. Looking at it, you see a curious design on the door.

If your {ROLLING STONE} is 5 or more, turn to **166** right now.

This is a puzzle!

A	A	B	A	177
C	B	B	C	206
A	B	C	A	191
B	A	B	C	192
191	178	193	?	

If you want to solve it, turn to the entry equal to the '?'. If the first words you see there are not *The locker creaks…*, take +1 {ROLLING STONE} and start this entry again.

If you just smash the locker open instead, turn to **121**.

125

You hear a low coughing noise as you're slammed sideways to reel down the corridor. You realize Deadpool pushed you. He has a gunshot wound in the center of his forehead. He sighs wearily, cracks his neck, and turns to a nearby classroom.

"Oh look, new friends," he says, and rolls into the room, guns flashing.

You peer in at an angle. It looks very much like a chemistry classroom. Folklore needs Bunsen burners and fume cabinets? Curious. A handful of smartly-dressed campus guards are ducking around the benches, snapping out to take suppressed-pistol potshots. Deadpool is just standing in the doorway, ignoring hits and apparently treating it as a game of shoot-a-mole. The guards are completely outclassed, which might be why he's mostly targeting gun-hands. Or he might just fancy the target practice. Hard to tell.

This is an easy fight.

Round one: roll two dice and add your **MERC**. If the total is at least equal to twice your {**GUARDS, GUARDS**} + 3, you win the first round.

Round two: roll two dice and add your **MERC**. If the total is at least equal to twice your {**GUARDS, GUARDS**}, you win the second round.

If you lost both rounds, turn to **187**.

If you won at least one round, turn to **80**.

126

It takes a while, but you find the only red warehouse on Clintonville Street. It's a squat concrete box in a squalid lot. There are a couple of anonymous-looking white trucks parked out front, and a number of cars nearby. They're just one step from the junkyard mostly, but you'd still take the worst of them over Deadpool's dreadful yellow shoebox – even the one littered with pizza boxes and stale milk cartons.

Deadpool watches the place while you daydream about comfortable knees. "It looks dead," he says finally. "In the boring way, not the fun way."

You're sure you'll regret it, but you have to ask. "The fun way?"

"Sure. The Addamses, the Munsters, Elvira. Didn't you ever see *Dracula's Dog*? Now *that* was a movie. José Ferrer upstaged by a mutt."

"I... guess? It's probably good that the warehouse isn't full of campy 1970s undead, though."

Deadpool sighs sadly. The front loading door is open and you could walk in, but you could also try round the back.

Sneak round the back? Turn to **122**.

Go in the front, turn to **71**.

127

Setting your cell phone to torch mode, you follow the draft into the darkness. A short walk brings you to a large, sheer-sided pit. Air blows out of it in gusts, laden with strange scents you can't identify, some acrid, others damp with organic decay. It's not horrible, oddly enough. Unidentifiable yellow sigils are painted all around the pit in a style you've never seen before. Deadpool is worryingly silent. You pick up a piece of rubble and toss it in, then wait.

You never hear the rubble land, but a faint, beckoning whispering starts. It's not using any words you recognize, but it urges you to join it, to become one. By Deadpool's cocked head, he hears it too.

To jump in, turn to **52**.

To pull away and follow the flow instead, turn to **118**.

128

Deadpool shrugs, pulls out his pistols, takes aim at the nearest suited minion, and looks at you. "Really?"

You nod, and he starts firing. Take +1 {DRAGONFIRE}.

This is a simple fight.

Round one: roll two dice and add your **MERC**. If the total is at least 9, you get them all. If not, progress to round 2.

Round two: roll two dice and add your **MERC**. If the total is at least 10, you pick them off before they can raise further alarms.

If you lost both rounds, you attracted attention: take +1 {DRAGONFIRE}.

Now, if you want to get onto the conveyor belt, turn to **230**.

If you want to advance on solid ground, turn to **174**.

129

The door to the white security room slams shut, and another door opens. Several guards come out, firing as soon as they're clear. You drop to the ground and slam your hands over your ears as Deadpool scythes his way through the nearest unfortunate.

Take +1 {DRAGONFIRE}.

This is a short, almost unfair fight.

Roll two dice and add your **MERC**. If the total is at least 10, you win.

The door the guards came through is a small barracks room, no way on. You head down the ladder in the middle of the room.

If you won, you're quick enough: turn to **83**.

If you lost, you're too slow: turn to **219**.

130

You open the door of The Hollow and walk in. It's as nasty inside as it is outside, all stained tables, cheap floor tiles, and faded photos on the wall of people who might have been somebody a few generations ago. There are maybe twenty guys inside, all of the big and muscular type. You see guns in waistbands, on tables, even a few in holsters. The bar is unpleasantly shiny, and behind it is a cheerful-looking young woman with bright purple hair and a Misfits T-shirt. All conversation stops dead, and everyone turns to stare at you: some with hostility, others with confusion.

Deadpool takes a breath.

"Hey," you say to him.

"Let's talk to the bartender." Turn to **261**.

"Let's start a fight." Turn to **229**.

"Let's try to scare them a bit." Turn to **158**.

131

"Wow. We're sneaking through an empty box into a smaller empty box. It's my dream come true, only Bea Arthur isn't here. What a waste. Nice footwork, Sixen. Very stealthy compared to The Thing."

You sneak into the staffroom despite Deadpool's running commentary. It's a dingy little space with a min-ifridge that's old enough to vote, but the bank of small lockers draws your eye. One has a suspiciously hi-tech keypad, complete with green LEDs. Above it, on the door, someone with appalling opsec habits has helpfully written, $8+12/4-3+6*7-5$.

If you type in *45*, turn to **272**.

If you type in *51*, turn to **49**.

If you type in *57*, turn to **254**.

132

You're in a stretch of dull corridor decorated with ancient movie posters. There's a security door, and as you're watching, it opens onto a pack of guards in three-piece suits – orange ones, this time. They're carrying serious military-grade automatic weapons, and they take cover in the doorway. Deadpool charges towards them, screaming a wild war-cry that you can't quite parse, but which might be something about horses. They fall back, opening fire as they go.

This is a moderately tough fight.

Round one: roll two dice, subtract your {WARNED}, and add your MERC and, if you have any, your {NAMES DOWN}. If the total is at least 13, you win the first round.

Round two: roll two dice, subtract your {WARNED}, and add your MERC and, if you have any, your {NAMES DOWN}. If the total is at least 13, you win the second round.

Round three: roll two dice, subtract your {WARNED}, and add your MERC and, if you have any, your {NAMES DOWN}. If the total is at least 13, you win the third round.

This fight is something of a running battle, and by the end

of it, there's a trail of dead. That's what they'll know you by.

If you won at least two rounds, Deadpool is fine. Take **+1 MOUTH**.

If you lost at least two rounds, Deadpool is less fine. Take **-1 MERC**.

Now, you're at a weirdly flickering intersection.

If you want to enter the server room, turn to **170**.

If you want to try the boiler room, turn to **116**.

133

Not quite believing what you're doing, you walk up to one of the building's walls and place your palms flat on it. Curious, Deadpool copies you. Remembering the horrifying whispers of the brain in the jar, you close your eyes and begin muttering a series of hideous sounds that burned themselves into the front of your mind. Your mind's eye hollows, becoming depthless and grotesque, and you know something is leering at you from Outside. Unlikely angles tear through your imagination. The world spins, and then everything is indescribable horror, a tittering, crawling chaos that makes a mockery of the joke you used to call physical reality. It lasts for ever and ever, an eternal moment of unfathomable madness.

Then you are in a hot, cramped, pitch-black space, jammed in with Deadpool. It feels like a cupboard. You are both weeping. There is nothing in existence that could make you do that again. You will die a thousand tortures first.

Take **-3 MOUTH, +2 FOCUS**, and **+1 {DISCORD}**.

To stay jammed in here and sob for a while, turn to **23**.

To force yourself up and out of your cupboard, turn to **290**.

134

A couple of seconds after Deadpool stops hammering on the door, it opens and an angry-looking transit official sticks her head out. "Sir..." Her brain catches up with the message her eyes are screaming to her, and the rest of her sentence vanishes.

"Hi!" Deadpool says. "You're Annie, right? Are you OK?"

Now she looks even more baffled. "Who? What?"

"There's a monster tunneling under New York right at this moment, Annie. A really big one. It's a bit like a T-Rex got crossed with a pill bug, specially adapted for burrowing. And death. Lots of death. It's coming for the subway system, I'm afraid. Will you let us in to save the day, or will you go down in history as the real monster here?"

A moment later, you're in the control room, watching as the woman whose name is not Annie sprints towards the controller's office.

Take **+1 MOUTH**.

The control room is an impressive sight. The walls are covered with highly technical data screens, and the floor area holds row after row of computer stations, equipment banks, and other large electronic bits. A dozen operators or more are working here, although most of them are looking over at you right now.

Deadpool waves at them, and most of them immediately look away. Then he turns to you. "The controller will be here any minute, Sixth Ave. Are we sticking with the lie, or should I..." He pats the gun on his hip. "Get physical?"

If you want to keep lying, turn to **180**.

If you want to try violence, turn to **264**.

135

You've seen this exact building in several paintings. Each time, there was a line of people in blue three-piece suits who were entering a small deli next door. Glancing at the lobby, you see lots of the same suits. Lunch choice, or something more?

You go to the lobby, which looks closed despite the

hour, but there's something suspiciously artificial about the ingredients on display. You try the door, and it is not locked. You file in, Deadpool following. There's a very big fridge at the end of the aisle between the counter and the window, and it's the only bright thing in here. You go over to the fridge and tug on the door. The whole thing slides forward and to one side, as smooth as silk.

"I should get one of these for the safe-house," Deadpool says.

"It would be your demise."

Deadpool shrugs and takes point, walking through a short, green-lit concrete tunnel and a more normal door into an office.

Take **+1 MOUTH** in bragging rights.

To exit the office through the door to the corridor, turn to **149**.

To head through a smaller door marked *Canteen*, turn to **290**.

136

"Why don't we try that alien gun?" you suggest.

"I like the way you think, Colonel Six. I knew there was something special about you." Deadpool fishes out the weapon, fiddles with it for a moment, then points it at the door.

There's a blast of indescribable light, a loud *foom*, and you have the horrible but fortunately brief sensation of ants crawling under your skin. Where the door was, there's now just a crater. The broken wall is bleeding molten steel. Electronic debris and suspicious traces of red mist fill the room beyond, which opens onto a short, blandly gray corridor.

There are doors to the left and the right.

To try the left door, turn to **222**.

To try the right door, turn to **27**.

137

The boxy storage building has no door, and the roof doesn't look like it's got long left either. You enter and, peering through a hole in the far wall, spy a crumbling hut a short way away. The floor is thick with dust, but there are big, oddly-clean patches, widely separated. No footsteps but your own. These patches have strange, irregular outlines, maybe even semi-organic. You can't imagine what made them. A stack of folded tarpaulin sheets is in the middle of a broad, molten-looking clean patch. Deadpool heads straight for the tarps.

"I'm not sure–" you start – then the ceiling collapses.

See if you can avoid this trap – roll one die, and add your **FOCUS** to it.

If you score 8 or more: Deadpool twists aside. Take **+1 MOUTH**.

7 or less: Deadpool is hit repeatedly. Take **-1 MERC** and **-1 MOUTH**.

To try the once-blue shed, go to **32**.

To check out the crumbling hut, go to **203**.

138

You're squeezed back into Deadpool's Yellow Mistake, heading over the Whitestone Bridge towards a safe-house he claims to have in Bushwick, a cool Hispanic district in Brooklyn. To your surprise, someone knocks on the window, hard enough to make the car jerk. Outside, matching your pace, is a huge guy wearing red metal-effect biker gear, driving an equally huge motorcycle. He waves for Deadpool to pull over.

You stop, and immediately car horns start blaring as other drivers are forced to acknowledge the existence of something outside themselves. The motorcycle stops behind you, and the pair of you get out.

Oh. It's not biker gear. It's some sort of exotic armor, that weird tapering dome isn't a bike helmet, and he's not just huge, he's a force of nature. You've seen a lot of very burly men and women in the last day or so, but this one just redrew the boundaries.

Juggernaut stomps over to meet you. He does not look happy. "Wilson, you freak. What in the six freaking hells is going on? I've been hearing a lot of really weird stuff, and you're in the middle."

"Jughead! Looking buff, big guy. Don't worry, Six, I've got this. Hammerhead's running a network of murderers, and there's these alien weapons, but it's all about money, and they've got – no, Six, it's okay, shh, shhhh – yeah, it's under the Ivy League, but they've been using black helicopters. There's a casino in Atlantic City, you know, and they've taken over that mutant school and turned it into a lair and day-spa, and–"

Make a babble test. Roll one die, and add your **MOUTH** to it.

If the total is 6 or more, Deadpool somehow alarms Juggernaut into attacking... something? He leaps onto his bike, and speeds off. Take **+1 {CHAOS}**.

If the total is 5 or less, Juggernaut lets Deadpool wind down, then shakes his head. "You're pathetic, Wilson. Completely broken." He gets on his bike and leaves, shaking his head in disgust all the way. Take **-1 MOUTH**.

Now it's time to prepare for the main event. You can call Weasel for some research first – but be warned, this will use up precious time – or you can go straight to the safe-house.

To research Hammerhead's core personnel, turn to **238**.

To research his network's operational structure, turn to **70**.

To head to the safe-house, turn to **216**.

139

You find yourself in a stretch of corridor. You can see a couple of security doors, one with a camera above it, the other accessible via a card reader. There's also a standard wooden door, and a few safely abstract artworks that pretend to decoration. Maybe Hammerhead's still in the process of getting the place set up properly.

If you have a [Security Pass], you can swipe it in the card reader by turning to **75**.

If you have [Disguises], you can use those to get past the camera by turning to **295**.

Otherwise, you'll just have to batter the wooden door down. – turn to **231**.

140

It turns out Deadpool knows a low-end but surprisingly comfortable bar just a couple of blocks away. It's nothing much to look at, but the drinks are cold, the snacks are salty, and Weasel is already there at the bar, waiting for you.

"Wade!" He stands up to perform a complex series of palm-slaps and other gestures with Deadpool. After thirty seconds, he groans. "Okay, you win this round. Six, how's it going?"

"Wonderful," you manage.

"I'm *sure* it is," he says. "First round is on Wade."

Take **+1 {FEELING GOOD}**.

If you have {GOOD DEED} at 1 or more, take **+1 MOUTH**.

Likewise, if you have {TERRIFYING WEASEL} a 1 or more, take +2 MOUTH.

Once – and only once – you may reduce one of MERC, MOUTH, or FOCUS BY -1 in return for either +2 MERC, +2 MOUTH, +2 FOCUS, or -2 {CHAOS}, or either -1 or +1 {DISCORD}. You cannot increase the same stat that you reduced.

Finally, Weasel offers Deadpool a little something for luck. If you like, you may take either a really cute [Kitten Photo] or an [Artisanal Stick Candy] – hand-rolled by unusually beautiful Central American women, if the label is to be believed.

You spend an hour at the bar, but eventually duty calls. Go back to the safe-house by turning to **216**.

141

It takes a few more minutes, but you spot a worker across an open stretch of concrete. You walk on over, hoping that the pair of you don't startle him as much as you did the gate guy. He looks up as you approach, and straightens, facing you. "Help you folks?"

Deadpool starts to say something, and you step forward quickly. "Hi. Yes, I hope so. Look, I know this is irregular, but..." You fish around and bring out a twenty, which you wave around unsubtly. "We're, uh, investigators. Has there been any particularly suspicious activity going on here in the last week or so I guess?"

The guy glances at the twenty. He looks unimpressed.

"Suspicious? We got a hundred-fifty thousand containers here. Hundreds of thousands of square feet of warehousing. Every last bit of it is suspicious in one way or another. Who you say you were? Investigators? Who for?"

You sigh, and find another fifty. There goes the book money. "We're looking for gun-runners," you say.

"They sound dangerous to cross," the guy says, and folds his arms.

"Extremely dangerous," Deadpool agrees. "Real animals. Cut you up as soon as look at you."

"Exactly," the guy says.

You look at Deadpool, stifling a sigh. "Do you have any money?"

"Sorry, Six. I never carry cash. I like to keep it simple."

You close your eyes for a moment, summoning strength. "I've got a total of–" You count it out. "Ninety-six dollars and forty-eight cents."

"Throw in that eWatch?" the guy asks.

"No!"

"Give him the watch," Deadpool says, with an encouraging nod. "It'll make you feel better. Set yourself free."

"Fine." You glare at the guy. "But you'd better not be wasting our time. These thugs might be dangerous, but my companion here is terrifying."

"Aww, thanks, Six! You're the best."

The dock worker takes your eWatch and your money, giving you back 23 cents. "Sweet watch. My daughter's gonna love it. Yeah, I know who you're talking about. They've got a small ship in break bulk down at the end of

Suez, and a nest of containers set up where Suez meets Marsh. Have fun storming the castle."

Take **+1 MOUTH**.

If you want to investigate the ship, turn to **96**.

If you want to investigate the containers, turn to **8**.

142

"This really is urgent, Mister Davies," you say. "Someone is smuggling alien guns into the city, and a lot of people might die if we don't stop it."

"It's true," Deadpool says seriously. "We really have to find these idiots."

The pilot nods, looking depressed. "They're going to destroy my Yelp rating, but yeah, okay."

He leads you to his helicopter, and ninety seconds later, you're hovering over New York, looking out at the famous skyline, wearing a headset.

Take **+1 FOCUS**.

"So where are we heading?" the pilot asks.

"Great question," Deadpool says. "Six?"

If you want to hunt for possibly suspicious aircraft, turn to **185**.

If you want to ask the pilot if he's seen anything odd, turn to **218**.

143

This room is a meditation space, with an actual carp pool containing, according to a small sign, the thirty-seven koi carp of wisdom. It smells real bad. There are benches around it though, so you stop for a moment to admire the fish.

Take **+1 FOCUS**.

    To go back to the corridor, turn to **24**.

    To head past the corridor, turn to **217**.

144

You walk to the water's edge. Deadpool was right: there's a small air pipe poking out from the water. "Fiery hole," he calls, unclips an advanced-looking grenade, and pops it into the pipe.

It rattles downward.

You wait.

Nothing happens.

Then some passing giant smashes you in the face with a tubful of water as the world lurches. You realize you can't hear anything, and the sky is lurching around disturbingly. Deadpool hauls you to your feet. He says something, but you've no idea what. All around you both, people are flailing and dashing around wildly. They're probably screaming. They certainly look like they're screaming. You unsteadily follow Deadpool back to the arcade through the chaos, and you are reassured to hear the glass smash as he kicks the door in. There's no one behind it, just a set of stairs heading down.

Take **+2 {CHAOS}** and **+1 {WET}**.

> Now, if you want to wait a minute to make certain no one is around, turn to **76**.
>
> If you want to press ahead before someone arrives, turn to **297**.

145

This was probably an office, but it's been completely emptied of furniture. That's because the three walls facing the door have been absolutely covered with photographs, maps, notes, photocopied documents, sometimes several layers deep. Lines of red string crisscross both the walls and the room in a baffling maze, linking various items.

Deadpool whistles. "*Someone's* gone crazy. You can trust me on that."

"Is this what Hammerhead's basing his hit list on?"

"Maybe? But that guy over there, the bald one next to the big eye thing, he sells newspapers in Queens. He's barely even the boss of his own lunch." He pulls out his phone and starts taking photos of everything. "I'm going to send these pics to Daredevil, along with some other bits and pieces. What? Turnabout is fair play, and anyway, he's the one who's used to going in blind."

Let's see how much intel you've gathered. What's your **{NAMES DOWN}** rating?

2 or more: Sweet – take **+1 MOUTH**.

1 or less: Sour – take **-1 MOUTH**.

Either way, take **+1 {NAMES DOWN}** now.

To go to the server room, turn to **170**.

To return to the disorientating intersection, turn to **75**.

146

You risk a few moments to examine the contents of some of the broken crates in the right-hand side of the warehouse. Most of it is consumables, like ration bars and boxes of rounds, but …

"Chitauri guns," Deadpool declares, holding up a futuristic shaved-down egg-shaped weapon. "And this." He throws you a device that looks a bit like a high-tech Rubik's cube had a baby with a very ugly squid.

"What the hell?"

"No idea."

You can take the **[Alien Device]** if you want.

"We should sabotage some guns," he says. "We might be on the receiving end some day."

It's easy enough, and the two of you spend five minutes sabotaging a few dozen weapons.

Take **+1 {NOBBLED GUNS}**.

If you now have three Alien items in your inventory, turn to **266**.

To investigate the left aisles, turn to **256**.

To scope out the shipping area you can see at the back, turn to **255**.

Head straight for the command suites? Turn to **232**.

147

You go into the staffroom, closing the door behind you. It's a dingy little space, with a microwave, some grudging coffee supplies, a minifridge that's old enough to vote, and a bank of small lockers. One of the lockers has a suspiciously hi-tech keypad in the middle of the door, complete with hints of green LED light. Above it, on the door, someone with appalling opsec has written in Sharpie: *8+12/4-3+6*7-5.*

"This is your speed, Hexxie," Deadpool says.

If you type in *45*, turn to **272**.

If you type in *51*, turn to **49**.

148

Coreham College is a beautiful campus university in the Collegiate Gothic style: red brick with white-trimmed arched windows, steeply gabled roofs, crenelated towers, and cupolas. It's set in several acres of carefully-kept grounds, lawns and groves punctuated with elegant paths and, here and there, fountains. It's busy with expensively-attired students bustling to and fro, many of whom are clutching books or toting heavy rucksacks.

"Hey! *Hey!* Deadpool!" You both look over at the excited shouting. A young man is rushing up, grinning widely. "Deadpool! It *is* you!"

Deadpool bows. "In the flesh."

"Omigod, I'm your biggest fan. I *have* to stab you in the face. Please, let me stab you in the face!"

Wait, what?

To let Deadpool get stabbed, turn to **5**.

To protest this senseless violence, turn to **94**.

149

You're in a normal-looking office corridor. Partition walls, foam tile ceiling, thin carpet flooring, the usual. It really isn't anything special – Hammerhead's obviously cheap. The doors are helpfully labeled with small metal plaques. The door at the end has glass windows, looking out onto a lobby which is absolutely seething with gun-toting goons in identical bright blue three-piece suits. They haven't noticed you yet. Deadpool eyes the lobby door. "The daycare looks fun."

To go into the lobby, turn to **85**.

To go into the office, turn to **6**.

To go into the canteen, turn to **290**.

To go into the break room, turn to **285**.

150

You head into the depths of SoHo. Deadpool leads you into a tiny rare book shop almost totally hidden in the basement beneath a shop selling antique pipes and pipe-racks. He ignores the bookseller in favor of a shelf of ancient, long-outdated IT manuals. After a moment of thought, he tugs on the shelf, which turns out to be built on a door. It swings open, and you both step through into a bright, modern-looking room bristling with weapons. There is a diverse spectrum of very menacing people behind the counter, like a united nations of gang members. Deadpool heads over and starts dickering.

Take **+2 MERC** and set {TOOLED UP} to 1.

After a little while, Deadpool comes over to you. "I've got a bunch of nice surprises here. I feel *good*. They offered me a sweetener – what do you think?"

You may, if you wish, take either a [Grenade] or a [Pointy Stick].

Afterwards, you return to the safe-house.

Turn to entry **216**.

151

Deadpool shrugs. "Nice. Right. They won't expect that." He walks over to a teller who accidentally lets their customer escape. "Ah, Collis, you're looking very sharp today. I love what you've done with your hair. It always brightens my day to see you behind the counter. Wait, did that come out wrong? I'd love for you to be free, like an osprey. You get that, right?"

The woman stifles a sigh. "How may I help, Mr Wilson?"

Take **+1 FOCUS** and **+1 {FLUSH}**.

It takes a while, but Deadpool eventually withdraws a small heap of cash, and you return to the safe-house. Turn to entry **216**.

152

A shotgun to the head at point-blank range will slow even Deadpool down for a while. Jengarm waves to the guards who carried in the table. "Slicer is ready in office. Push him in quickly. First head. Separate slices with metal plates and feed to pigs in basement, no more than three each. Kill pigs immediately and dump at sea for sharks. By time he rebuilds from fish-guano on ocean floor and crawls out, is much too late." He pauses, and turns to look at you. "As for you, companion of Deadpool, you will be useful. You like… games, I hope."

Everything goes black.

ACHIEVEMENT: *Sleeping With The Fishes*.

The end.

153

"Be scary," you mutter to Deadpool.

You can sense his grin. "I love it!"

The receptionist is here now. "May I ask what it going on?"

Deadpool growls. "You are all going to *die*. A wave of horrifying violence will engulf the USA, leading to a new terrorist empire controlling the country with a brutal fist, and it is. All. Your. Fault." He yells the last few words in a menacing rockslide howl.

Take +1 {CHAOS}.

Did he persuade her? Roll one die and add your MERC.

Score of 8 or more: The receptionist calls for experts, who take Deadpool very seriously. Take +2 {WEAPONS DOWN}.

7 or less: The receptionist sighs, and ten seconds later, the pair of you are pitched out of the office and told not to come back.

Either way, return to the safe-house by turning to **216**.

154

The pair of you head out, and into the heart of the Bronx. Deadpool takes you to a small jokes and novelties store wedged between a decent-looking deli and a really avant garde art gallery – the current exhibit appears to be a featureless white ceramic cube, one foot to a side, suspended five feet in the air.

You go in, and wait as Deadpool browses a range of

things typically associated with eight year-olds, like stink-bombs and palm buzzers.

Take **+2 MOUTH** and **+1 {ZANY}**.

His arms laden with cheap gags, Deadpool wanders over. "I was wondering if you thought I should get one of these?" He shows you a **[Rubber Chicken]** and a **[Clown Mask]**. You may add one of these to your inventory, if you wish.

He buys the heap of toys from a very bored-looking teenager, and then you return to the safe-house. Turn to **216**.

155

The construction workers don't want to hand over an earth-mover until Deadpool pulls a gun. Then, unsurprisingly, they're only too happy to help.

You clamber in. Deadpool fires up the machine, whooping and hollering in delight, and you head straight towards an unbroken stretch of wall. You just have time to think about bracing for impact before there's an almighty crash, a riot of falling masonry, and your teeth rattle painfully in your skull.

But is this the right place? Make an accuracy test. Roll one die and add your **FOCUS**.

Score of 6 or more: It's not obviously wrong, at least. Take **+1 {CHAOS}** and turn to **177**.

5 or less: No, the bank doesn't extend this far. You're looking through the brick dust at a traumatized dentist, dental assistant, and tooth patient. Oops. Take **+2 {CHAOS}** and flee back to **216**.

156

You watch as Deadpool strides over the fallen guards towards the professor at the back of the room. "Hi, honey," he says. "I'm home!"

The professor scowls, and lifts up a Chitauri gun. "Come no closer."

Do you have a {NOBBLED GUNS} score of 1 or more, or a [Razor-Ball]?

If you have {NOBBLED GUNS} of 1 or more, the professor tries to fire, but nothing happens.

If you have a [Razor-Ball], you pull it out and hold it up, and the professor immediately goes pale and lowers his gun.

If you don't have either, the professor fires, and a beam of ravening energy envelops Deadpool. Take -4 MERC. If that leaves you at MERC 0 or less, Deadpool is burned away to nothing. **The end.**

Assuming you're not below 1 MERC, Deadpool shakes his head, and advances. The professor shrieks, throws his gun across the room, and curls up in a ball in his chair. "No! Don't hurt me! Please, you can't hurt me. I'm too important to die!"

"You really aren't," Deadpool says.

"What?"

"You're barely even a walk-on. I could eradicate you from existence and no one would even remember you'd ever existed. You're a convenience, nothing more. It's pathetic, honestly."

"What?" the professor repeats. He looks wild-eyed.

"I'll make it simple," Deadpool says. "Tell me what I need to know."

"And you'll let me live?"

"Do goldfish eat radioactive shrimp?"

Apparently, that's good enough. "I'm working for Hammerhead, okay. He set this whole thing up. Flood the nation's crime networks with fake Chitauri guns made in a facility in Brazil."

"Why Brazil?"

"It's really cheap. The guns go on sale everywhere tomorrow, just expensive enough not to cause suspicion. We're claiming it's just a few. Everyone will grab them, because they'll be scared their competition will buy them. Then, as chaos descends, we deactivate the guns and assassinate the leadership of every criminal organization in the nation."

"That's unlikely."

"We've got an incredible hit-list, if I say so myself. The big ones, the little ones, the tiny flyspeck ones, the bike gangs, the Italians, the Russians, everyone. That's my department. I know every active criminal in the country. Teams are ready in every city. What with all the collateral death, and the national horror at this incredible massacre, the police will be on the warpath."

"Worse, you'll have Spider-Man out there being all sanctimonious."

"Quite. It will be deeply problematic for the gangs. Then our people will sweep in, gather up the traumatized lieutenants and other surviving low-end command personnel, and tell them Hammerhead will make all their problems go away – but they work for him now. It's all arranged so that Wilson Fisk appears to be behind the guns, so once everything is in order, we will leak some documents and let Fisk be hunted. In short order, Hammerhead will be running all the crime in the entire USA. Except Hawai'i, but that place is a warzone."

"It is?"

"Don't you watch television? Anyway, phase four is to unify the criminal structure of America into one truly magnificent hive, an empire of crime like the world has never seen before outside of politics. It's going to be... Ah. Hm." He makes a visible effort to stop gloating. "That is, it's an ambitious plan, but I'm certain you can stop it. Hammerhead's in the new Meteorite Building in New York. Go, ah, get him." The professor winds down, huddling there miserably.

Deadpool looks at you. "Hammerhead is completely guano-flinging crazy. We've got to stop him, Six. Flooding the country with Chitauri guns is bad enough. Putting him in charge of crime would be a disaster. It'd make Hydra look like a terrifying, ruthlessly evil fascist conspiracy to enslave the world and drag it into a new dark age."

ACHIEVEMENT: *Crème of the Crop*.

There's a [Crowbar] on the floor that you may take if you like, but there's nothing more to do here. Time to head back to New York.

If you want to recap what you've learned so far, turn to **68**.

If you'd rather skip the exposition, turn to **28**.

157

This room is filled with cardboard boxes, at least sixty-six of them. Deadpool opens one at random, to reveal a big stack of printed records. They don't appear to make much sense. You may take an [Encrypted File] if you wish.

Make a spot hidden things test. Roll one die, and add your FOCUS to it.

Score of 6 or more: Behind some boxes, you find a [Tiger Amulet]. If you take it, you may at some future point destroy it to automatically pass any one stealth test.

To go back to the corridor, turn to 24.

To head past the corridor, turn to 217.

158

Deadpool does something impressive with his swords and drops into a combat-ready stance, looking pointedly at all of the guns. "Hi. I'm Deadpool. I don't know if you know this, but bullets are not exactly a problem for me. Anyone who isn't ready to die in screaming agony should really get out of here right now."

Take an intimidation test. Roll one die, and add your MERC to it. What is the total?

Score of 6 or more: A bunch of guys look at each other nervously, then hurry out the doors. Turn to 220.

5 or less: Yeah… no, that one just didn't land. Turn to 229.

159

You're past all the tricks, traps, and mooks, in the very fancy elevator that goes up to Hammerhead's lair. This is your last chance to get Deadpool's head as straight as it goes.

If you want, take **+1 {WARNED}** in order to swap 1 or 2 points between your **MERC**, **MOUTH**, or **FOCUS** scores. You can do this more than once if you have the points.

For a recap of what you've discovered, turn to **184**.

To visit Hammerhead's lair, turn to **271**.

160

Deadpool tugs on the door. It opens easily and as it does, a burst of machine-gun fire echoes through the room. Screams erupt all around you, in the auction room as well as others further off. Deadpool pulls out his pistols as a pack of guards floods out – thirty or more.

This is a tough fight. Take **+1 {CHAOS}**.

Round one: roll two dice and add your **MERC**. If the total is at least 10, you win the first round.

Round two: roll two dice and add your **FOCUS**. If the total is at least 9, you win the second round.

If you won both rounds, turn to **247**.

If you lost any rounds, turn to **109**.

161

The admin building is spectacular on the outside, but inside it's as brown and depressing as any administration area you've seen. The counter has places for four attendants, but all of them are empty.

"Hell-o-o?" Deadpool calls. "We need some help here! Hi? Don't worry, it's safe, I'm not one of those students. I'm actually a super hero on a mission of life or death. You can check me out on YouTube. Hello? It'll only take a moment of your time. It's very simple. Is there anyone there? I love what you've done with the place. Dentist chic."

A small, sour-faced woman dawdles into view. She's not the most intimidating thing you've seen recently, but it's close. Deadpool starts to say something, but she *tutts* him quiet. Finally she arrives, and Deadpool begins to talk again, but she holds up a finger, fidgeting around with papers on her desk.

By the time she looks up, Deadpool's wandered off in one corner having a burbled conversation with a large aspidistra. She pointedly ignores him to glare lasers at you. "What?"

"Professor Hope?" you ask.

Make a persuasion test. Roll one die, and add your **MOUTH** to it.

On a score of 8 or more: she sniffs and points to a building on a map on the counter. Turn to **209**.

7 or less: she stands, turns around, and shuffles off.

Despite Deadpool's best attempts to irritate her back into view, she does not return. Take +1 {GUARDS, GUARDS}, and try the library instead. Turn to **299**.

162

You and Deadpool leap eagerly into the abyss, but you fall through the pitch darkness alone – and fall, and fall, and fall. Eternities pass. That which was you discovers awareness of shapes in the darkness, invisible but still somehow perceivable. They writhe and intermingle in a thousand forms, hard blocks, darting arrows, puffy congeries, formless abominations, nonexistent stars, putrid cylinders, on and on. Over the eons, nightmares whisper secrets to you, secrets that would change all of life itself. You will never get to transmit them however, for you have passed outside of all time and space, and there is no coming back.

ACHIEVEMENT: *A Million Lemmings*.

The end.

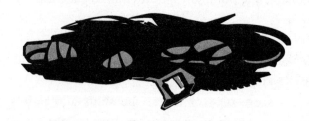

163

You study the circuit board behind the panel. It needs you to pick out a path across a maze of nodes in order to power something.

This is a number maze puzzle.

If you have a [Magnifying Glass], or you just want to give up, turn to 267.

Starting at a "1" in the top row, move to a vertically or horizontally adjacent "3", then a "5" a "7", a "9", and back to a "1" again. Keep moving to adjacent squares, always following the repeating pattern 1> 3> 5> 7> 9> 1> 3> etc, until you reach the bottom.

TOP

9	3	7	1	3	1	3	9	1	5	7	1
7	5	1	3	5	3	7	5	3	9	1	3
5	3	9	5	7	9	3	9	5	7	3	5
3	1	3	1	9	5	1	7	3	9	1	7
1	9	7	5	3	1	9	3	1	7	3	1
9	5	9	3	7	5	7	5	9	3	5	7
5	9	1	7	5	3	1	3	1	9	7	1
7	7	3	5	3	1	7	1	5	3	5	9
3	9	1	7	1	5	3	7	9	3	1	5
1	3	1	9	3	7	9	1	3	5	7	3
5	5	7	1	3	5	3	7	5	1	9	1
3	9	3	5	7	3	7	1	7	3	7	9

BOTTOM

When you know the route, total up all the numbers in it, then add 99 and turn to that entry. If the first words are not *The panel lights up*, you'll have to come back here and try again.

164

There are hundreds of slot machines, captivating dozens of spray tan disaster victims who escaped from the set of a zombie apocalypse movie. You have a vision of people on beds being sucked dry of fluids by evil movie scientists.

If you have {TIPSY} of 1, you can't resist, and must play. You can still choose to play if you are sober, of course.

This is a predatory minigame!

Exchange one of your inventory items (or take -2 MOUTH) for 5 credits.

Pay 1 credit, then roll two dice.

If you get 6 and 6, add 16 credits.

If the first die is a 6 and the second is not, add 3 credits.

If you get 1 and 1, add 2 credits.

Otherwise, you get nothing. You can play again or stop.

You can buy back your original item (but not the MOUTH penalty) for 8 credits, and if you get to 36 credits, you can buy the [Glittering Prize]. Pick one of MERC, MOUTH, or FOCUS: it temporarily adds 2 to that stat while carried.

Now, to head to the bar, turn to **270**.

To investigate the auction, turn to **262**.

165

You walk over to the Straczinsky poster. Something about the way it's lying against the wall makes you suspicious. You take it down, and sure enough, there's a small nook built into the wall behind it. You reach in, and find a pair of [Adamantium Knuckles]. While they're in your inventory, increase your MERC by +2. Take +1 {PUZZLER}.

ACHIEVEMENT: *Secret Hunter One*. Congratulations!

Now, to research One Family, Inc, turn to **175**.

To head straight over to Central Park, turn to **48**.

166

Unfortunately, you're out of time. You hear a hiss, and look up. Uh-oh. Gas? You try to hold your breath, but the world goes fuzzy, and you slump to the ground.

Turn to **33**.

167

Juggernaut and Deadpool square off, and traffic grinds to a halt as people abandon cars and flee. Deadpool dances in to attack. Juggernaut grabs him by the head, and slams him into the concrete like he was a wet rag. He aims a punch down, but Deadpool somehow rolls out of the way. The bridge creaks. Then the fight really starts.

This is a hard boss fight. Take +2 {CHAOS}.

Round one: roll three dice and add your MERC and

MOUTH, as Deadpool tries to goad Juggernaut into accidentally crushing a car. If the total is at least 18, you win the first round.

Round two: roll three dice and add your **FOCUS** and **MOUTH**. Deadpool really wants Juggernaut to punch through the bridge and fall in. If the total is at least 18, you win the second round.

Round three: roll three dice and add your **MERC** and **FOCUS**, as Deadpool tries to maneuver Juggernaut near to the edge of the bridge. If the total is at least 18, you win the third round.

Round four: roll three dice and add your **MOUTH** twice, as a badly-injured Deadpool infuriates Juggernaut into charging him on the bridge railings. If the total is at least 18, you win the fourth round.

Juggernaut plunges into the East River, still swearing, as Deadpool totters over to wave weakly.

If you lost 2 or more rounds, take **-4 MERC**.

If you won 3 or more rounds, take **-2 MERC**.

If your **MERC** is now 0 or less, set it to a very injured 1.

ACHIEVEMENT: *The Bridgeburners.*

Now it's time to prepare for the main event. You can call Weasel for some research first – but be warned, this will use up precious time – or you can go straight to the safe-house.

> To research Hammerhead's core personnel, turn to **238**.
>
> To research his network's operational structure, turn to **70**.
>
> To head to the safe-house, turn to **216**.

The office trailer looks dismal, but you go in, and are surprised to see hints of recent use. There's little dust, and papers that are not molded over. The chairs look like instruments of torture, all weird angles and folded planes, but they're set in front of sturdy desks. Several of the documents are in some swirly, unsettling fake alphabet, but there's also a map of the northeast USA. Your current location is highlighted with a five-pointed star.

"You are here?" you suggest.

"More like 'You are in deep–'"

"No," you say quickly. "We are in deep safety and calm."

He barks a quick laugh. "Sure thing, Six-shooter. Deep safety." He tosses the map down.

Make a luck test. Roll one die.

If you get 4 or more, the map's landing disturbs a [Creepy Ball]. If you take it, you can use it once to change any one die roll to "6".

Out the back, you see a couple of new structures.

To try the blue-flecked shed, turn to **32**.

To examine the oddly clean outhouse, turn to **198**.

169

A slightly off-color panel in the service corridor wall gives way under your touch, opening onto a hidden cupboard. Most impressive!

Take **+2 MERC** and **+1 MOUTH**, and the **ACHIEVEMENT**: *Secret Hunter Three*.

On the shelf, you see a **[Timebomb]**. If you take it, you can use it at any time – even at "**The end**" – to reset all your primary stats to 3, your **{CHAOS}** to 4, and all your other secondary qualities to 0, then jump to **48**. Could prove useful!

Now move on past the service corridor and turn to **217**.

170

The server room is large, dark, cold, and packed with row after row of computer racks. LEDs flick on and off, throwing up strange momentary shadows. It's difficult to hear anything over the humming of all those cooling systems.

Deadpool drops into a roll, shooting forward beneath a large shining blade that tried to spear him from out of the gloom. There's more humming, and some sort of security robot comes into view. It's like a sturdy pillar, bristling with blades and sensors. A black logo that reads *ACNOTEC, Inc* is spread across it.

This is a short, nasty fight.

If you have an **[FBI Badge]**, the robot scans it and shuts down. Third party vendors...

Otherwise, you'll need to roll two dice, subtract your {WARNED}, and add your MERC.

If the total is 11 or less, Deadpool is hacked up painfully during the fight – take -1 MERC and -1 FOCUS.

With the robot stopped, you can study the machinery and the operator terminal.

If you have a [USB Key], remove it from your inventory to take -2 {WARNED}.

Otherwise, make a hacking test. Roll one die and add your FOCUS and your MOUTH.

On a score of 14 or more: -2 {WARNED}.

10-13: Nothing happens.

9 or less: You make it worse. +1 {WARNED}.

If your {WARNED} is now less than 1, set it back to 1.

Now, if you want to go into the adjacent room, turn to **145**.

If you want to try the boiler room, turn to **116**.

To return to the disorientating intersection, turn to **75**.

171

Heading up the stairs, you come fairly quickly to a mezzanine landing. There's only one door here, a sturdy-looking one marked *SECURITY*. You can hear a faint hubbub through the door. Risky...

If you want to go into Security, turn to **82**.

If you want to go on up the stairs, turn to **132**.

172

Deadpool nods. "You bet, amigo." He walks over to a teller who accidentally lets their customer escape. "Did you know that there's a species of spider that lays its eggs in your eyes while you're on the toilet? It's a really big problem in Atlanta. The eggs are really small, but they're surprisingly loud, and they make it tough to get a good night's sleep. They don't hatch, they just dissolve in the eye, but by that time you've got some more in there. A whole city with egg-eye, never getting a decent rest. The whole place is totally exhausted. Spider-Man told me all about it and let's face it, he'd know. He bred those spiders himself. Those poor people."

The woman stifles a sigh. "How may I help, Mr. Wilson?"

Take **+1 MOUTH** and **+1 {FLUSH}**.

It takes a while, but Deadpool eventually withdraws a small heap of cash, talking about spiders all the way, and you return to the safe-house. Turn to **216**.

173

This room is a medium-sized barracks, with bunk beds providing sleeping space for twenty-four people. A small group of guards in expensive suits are sitting around a couple of the beds, playing dice. They look up as you enter, reaching for weapons.

Take **+1 {DRAGONFIRE}**

This is an easy fight.

Round one: roll two dice and add your **MERC**. If the total is at least 8, you win the first round.

Round two: roll two dice and add your **MERC**. If the total is at least 7, you win the second round.

If you lose both rounds, a lucky shot blinds one of Deadpool's eyes until it regrows. Ouch, stinger. Take **-1 MERC**.

To go back to the corridor, turn to **24**.

To head past the corridor, turn to **217**.

174

You walk on through the records storage cellar. The enemies around you are far too busy to even acknowledge you. Can you even call them enemies?

Apparently you said that out loud. "You can call anyone an enemy," Deadpool says reassuringly. "Try it. It's fun!" The boss is up on the conveyor belt, near the shredder's mouth. Deadpool walks over and looks up. "Hi. We have some questions."

The big man looks down. "You are who, in the name of the devil?" His voice sounds a bit like a choir of angels put through a horrible robotic voice-changer.

"Deadpool and the Six."

"Be away. This is busy now."

Deadpool tilts his head to one side. "Did it hurt when you fell out of the toilet? Or was it a tragic teleport accident with a monkfish?" The minions are going pale at Deadpool's words, and trying to edge away without stopping work. "Wait, I think I knew your mother, up in Alaska. Nell, right? You could be my son. Come on, big boy, call me Daddy!"

Make an annoyance test. Roll one die, and add your **MOUTH** to it.

Score of 7 or more: turn to **108**.

6 or less: turn to **230**.

175

Deadpool takes you a cruddy bar hidden inside a depressing tenement. The people you pass seem to recognize him, at least. A ferrety little nerd guy is behind the bar, and he looks up as you come in. "Wade! What'll it be."

"Hey, Weas. Your roughest vermouth poured over a pint of smashed lemon wedges with black pepper for my new friend, and a vodka."

The guy whips up your appalling drink, and puts it in front of you. "You'd better drink it," he whispers, sounding scared. "Wade can get real tetchy. Like just absolutely gruesome. Pull your guts out through your mouth, turn you upside down, grab a can of gas and fill your–"

"Weasel!" Deadpool says. "Where's mine?"

He shrugs and puts the vodka on the bar. "Which one is this, then?"

"Six," Deadpool says.

"Already? What happened to, like, Three, Four, and Five?"

Deadpool shrugs. "Who cares? I did like Two."

"Oh yeah," Weasel says. "Two was amazing. Those eyes…"

"Remember those eyes the way you saw them, old buddy. Enjoy that. So much better."

Weasel looks over. "Aw, don't worry. We're just joking around, right, Wade?"

"Sure," Deadpool says. "Joking around. You're absolutely the first wildly unqualified person I've ever dragged into a ridiculously dangerous scheme, Six. Do you know how to skydive? Wait, don't answer that."

"So what do you lovebirds actually need?" Weasel asks.

"One Family, Inc. They've got an office on Bethesda Terrace in Central Park, somehow. What can you find out?"

Make a research test for Weasel. Roll one die, and add your **MOUTH** to it.

Score of 7 or more: turn to **7**.

6 or less: turn to **278**.

176

The locker creaks... and that's it. We mean, come on. Either you're here because you're flipping through randomly, or you solved the puzzle and then deliberately went to the entry that was four times A, instead of the correct one. Smartypants.

Take **+2 MOUTH**, but also **-1 FOCUS**.

You hear a hiss, and look up. Uh-oh. Gas? You try to hold your breath, but the world goes fuzzy, and you slump to the ground.

Turn to **33**.

177

Leaving all the mess behind you, you enter the vault. The one thing your research couldn't tell you was the form of wealth that was being kept here.

If you have a **[Sparkling Icosahedron]**, good on you. Can't beat a nice shiny d20. It bends chance for you – turn to **38**.

Otherwise, make a luck test. Roll one die to find out what the vault holds.

Roll a 1 or 2: Paper cash. Turn to **236**.

3-4: Gold. Turn to **111**.

5-6: Servers with access to electronic accounts. Turn to **38**.

178

"We should try to cripple their finances. If they can't pay, they'll be a lot weaker."

"Ooh, a bank job. I haven't robbed a bank in, oh, minutes. How exciting! Where are we raiding?"

That's a good question, one that will take some research to answer.

Take **+1 {OUT OF TIME}**.

Now make a research test: Roll one die, and add your **FOCUS**, and if you have any, your **{ORG SEC}** and your **{RESOURCEFUL}**.

Total of 8 or more: You find a likely target. Go to **102**.

7 or less: The time is wasted. Go back to **216**.

"If I wanted to keep my smuggling really secret, maybe I'd keep underground," you suggest.

"Ooh, dirty tunnels. I like it." He fires up the car and takes off without the slightest attention to the surrounding traffic. A black sedan veers wildly to avoid getting rammed, and you catch a glimpse of a furious-looking business person. "If I was going down there, I'd want to make sure I wasn't making any nasty mistakes, you know? It can get real brutal. And you know what that means."

"I genuinely don't," you say.

"It means Penn Station. That's where they have the control room for the entire network."

You sigh in relief. "The subway."

"Yes," he says with exaggerated patience. "The subway. I went there with Beast once, but hopefully they've forgotten. If anyone is using the subway to move shipments, Penn control is where we'll find out about it."

Despite Deadpool's terrifying driving, it still takes fifty minutes to travel the three miles to Penn Station, although twenty of that is hunting the streets for one particular fried burrito cart. Parking is surprisingly easy, because he just rams the tiny yellow blob into the back of a much better car and forces it forwards until it's jammed into the one in front.

Penn Station is as much a maze of claustrophobic concrete brutalism as you remember, broken up now with an occasional splash of light, airy concourse to impart a false sense of hope. You're quickly lost, but Deadpool terrorizes the first employee he sees into serving as his guide. Eventually, this wild-eyed unfortunate leads you to a stretch of corridor several levels underground. He points to a huge pair of frosted glass doors with *Control Center* stenciled on them, then turns and sprints off into the gray wilds.

Deadpool watches them go. "Some people are just squirrely," he says. "Don't take it personally, Six. I know how great you are."

You shake your head. He pats you on the shoulder, then walks up to the doors, and tries them. They don't open, so he starts yelling "Hey!" and hammering on them rhythmically. After about half a minute of this, he turns to you. "Someone's coming. Quick. How should I play this?"

If you think honesty is the best policy, turn to **34**.

If you want to try a plausible lie, turn to **134**.

If you want Deadpool to use force, turn to **16**.

180

The controller hurries over towards the two of you, looking nervous but resolute. She's a stern-faced woman in her fifties, clearly not someone to be trifled with.

Deadpool goes to meet her. "I'm sorry," he tells her. "There's a monster coming for the subway network. It's huge, with an armored shell, razor claws, hideous breath, just absolutely vile. CR20 at least. It tunnels through stone as easily as fish swim through water. Someone is doing something naughty in the subway with alien power sources, and it's homing in on them. It's going to devour everything. The whole city maybe."

She doesn't look convinced. In the background, you notice a greasy little guy glare at you, and scuttle out.

"We have to find where the alien power supplies are being hidden. Right now. Our only chance is to catch it there. You have to help."

Test your **MOUTH** – roll one die, and add your **MOUTH** to it. What is the total?

5 or more: turn to **196**.

4 or less: turn to **277**.

181

You do your best to make your voice sound menacing. "We don't have to *completely* kill him. Does he need both those ears?"

"You know, that's a great question." There's a blur, and

one of Deadpool's swords is against the pilot's head, the blade resting along the top of his left ear. "*Do* you need both of these?"

Robert has gone as white as a sheet. "I'll take you up immediately, sir."

Take **+1 MERC**.

Ninety seconds later, you're up in the sky, wearing a headset and looking out over the familiar New York City skyline. The pilot is shaking and muttering, and occasionally he flinches at nothing, but he's keeping the helicopter still.

Deadpool looks out the window, peering about carefully. "Is that a banded kestrel? Wait, is a banded kestrel even a real bird?"

"They're from Madagascar?" Robert sounds terrified.

"I loved that movie," Deadpool says. "Those penguins were hilarious."

Apparently it's up to you to get things back on track.

If you want to hunt for possibly suspicious aircraft, turn to **185**.

If you want to ask the pilot if he's seen anything odd, turn to **218**.

182

The metro system is closed, but Deadpool gets you in through the simple strategy of cutting a door in the metal grating. If anyone hears him, they very wisely decide it's probably someone else's problem. You pass through the eerie tunnels to the platforms. "Last time I was down here like this, I met a girl called Cynthia. That was quite something, let me tell you. The ghosts, though..."

"Ghosts?"

"A word of advice, pre-Seven. Don't anger a ghost." Deadpool leaps off the platform and onto the rails. There's a flash of blinding light, a sudden stench of roast hero, clouds of smoke, and a wild shriek. A moment later, he stumbles out of the smoke and clambers back onto the platform, coughing heavily and looking toasty around the edges. "Watch out for that," he says. "Ghosts and electricity. Can't have the latter without the former."

You walk nervously off the end of the platform and down the tunnel, staying well away from the rails. From the glances he gives them, you suspect Deadpool is considering another dose. You find the door, set in a small alcove, with surprising ease, and go on through.

Test your luck. Roll one die.

If you roll a 3-6, turn to **51**.

Roll a 1-2, turn to **76**.

183

Despite Deadpool's best efforts, the boss clearly feels he has the advantage up on the belt, as he refuses to be thrown off. During one wild exchange, you see why: his big toes are prehensile, and he's got a strong grip on the sides of the belt casing. Deadpool has to keep dancing back, and his footing is dreadful by comparison. After some ineffectual swipes, he closes and attempts to wrestle the man. It is not a good idea.

If you have a **[Large Metal Block]**, that's solid enough to gum up the woodchipper, fusing the belt and giving Deadpool the chance to take the fight to ground level. Turn immediately to **108**.

If not, you'll have to try to get the boss off the belt the hard way. This is a tricky fight.

Round one: roll three dice and add your **MERC**. If the total is at least 12, you win the first round.

Round two: roll three dice and add your **FOCUS**. If the total is at least 12, you win the second round.

Round three: roll three dice and add your **MERC**. If the total is at least 12, you win the third round.

> If you won at least two rounds, Deadpool manages to dislodge the boss and move the fight to the ground. Turn to **108**.
>
> If you lost at least two rounds, turn instead to **197**.

184

So, Hammerhead has stockpiled alien weapons all over the USA. Tomorrow, he unleashes a tide of assassinations to kill all the ranking gang heads in the country. Then he'll sweep in and take over, unifying American crime into a horrifying empire. You've got to help Deadpool stop him. Any questions? (Please don't ask us questions. We can't hear you.)

To take five and think this over some more, turn to **159**.

To go to Hammerhead's lair, turn to **271**.

185

You give it some thoughts. "Let's fly around for a while, look for unscheduled flights or traffic in unusual places."

The pilot shrugs, but obediently starts flying around the city.

"Let us know if anything unfamiliar stands out," you tell him. Deadpool snickers.

Twenty minutes later, you've had a nice flight around New York, but you don't appear to be any closer to any smugglers. "What's that?" Deadpool says, pointing to a news copter.

"It's a news copter," the pilot says.

"Suspicious!" he says.

"Not really," says the pilot.

"What about that black helicopter over there?"

"That's..." The pilot trails off. "Actually, that's unmarked. That is genuinely suspicious."

"Maybe that's too obvious," Deadpool says. "Which is it, Six?" Apparently "neither" isn't an option, but you might as well get closer to one or the other.

"I think they're sneaky. Let's try the news copter." Turn to **100**.

"I think they're arrogant. Let's try the black copter." Turn to **29**.

186

"Let's just attack it," you find yourself saying.

"Ah, senseless violence. My favorite." He pulls out a grenade, primes it, and flings it at the door. The pair of you duck back into the steam tunnels for a moment. There's a ridiculously loud blast that you're sure you hear in your spleen, and then he's heading back in.

The lobby area is annihilated, and the door leading on is hanging drunkenly on one hinge. The wood paneling has been blown to splinters, and you can see the vault steel beneath. Deadpool grabs the broken door and heaves, and it topples to reveal a very angry looking guy with a very big machine-gun.

This is a simple fight.

Round one: roll two dice and add your **MERC**. If the total is at least 10, you win the first round.

Round two: roll two dice and add your **MERC**. If the total is at least 7, you win the second round.

If you lose either or both rounds, during the fight, a burst of machine-gun fire almost chews a hole in Deadpool's torso. Take **-1 MERC**.

When the shooting is over, the guard lies dead with bullet holes in both eyes and stitching a crooked smile across his face. Past him is a small room with a number of enigmatic, code-filled terminal displays which opens onto a short, blandly gray corridor. There are doors to left and right.

To try the left door, turn to **222**.

To try the right, turn to **27**.

187

A couple of lucky shots knock Deadpool down briefly, and the single uninjured guard seizes the chance to work him over with his pistol-butt, cursing savagely with each blow. Eventually, he stalks off to get help for his buddies, whose hands really hurt.

Beaten up by a guy who's barely more than a mall cop. It's colossally embarrassing, a new low in a long career of looking for new lows. Deadpool is mortified, and refuses to even talk about it. His mood only improves a little when he notices that a hole in a fume hood is venting chlorine – mustard gas – into the campus.

Take **-1 MERC**, **-1 MOUTH**, and **+2 {CHAOS}**.

You cross the corridor to Professor Hope's office and knock.

"Enter," says an impatient, plummy voice. Deadpool

pushes the door open and strides in. "Oh, look, a fool and his puppy." The professor is in his late fifties, sleek and well-groomed, with the face of a jaded Victorian esthete run to seed. He waves you away disgustedly. "Go back to Mirocaw or Carcosa or whatever you think you're doing, and let me work."

Deadpool walks up to the big, plush oak desk, and leans on it. "My name is Deadpool. We need to ask–"

"I don't care." The professor sits up a little straighter, and flips a switch in one arm of his desk chair.

A claxon sounds momentarily, the door slams shut, and the professor – and his chair – vanish back into a gaping hole where a bookcase had been a moment before. Then everything lurches, and the section of floor you're on plummets down into the ground.

When it lurches to a stop, you're in a room with solid metal walls, broken only by a heavy looking steel security door.

If you have a **[Sledgehammer]** and want to use it, turn to **69**.

To crawl through an air vent, turn to **234**.

To smash through the door, turn to **296**.

188

It's getting close to the end of the working day. "I've got an idea," you tell Deadpool.

You don't even need to make any phone calls, not any more. In twenty minutes flat, the pizzas start rolling in to One Family, all for "Mike," and they Just. Keep. On. Coming. When there's a whole crowd at the front of the door, you take the boxes from one relieved delivery guy – you have the receipt on your phone, after all – and push on through.

The guards behind the door are completely overwhelmed, and you're not the only people rushing past them. One glances at Deadpool. "Hey!"

"I'm from SuperPizza," Deadpool says quickly. "Pies for heroes, by heroes, tasting of heroes. Tee-Emm brackets. Arr brackets. Pat pending."

While the guards are processing this, you push on down the stairs behind them.

Make a persuasion test. Roll one die, and add your **MOUTH** to it.

Score of 5 or more: turn to **51**.

4 or less: turn to **76**.

189

The dumb waiter is a king-sized coffin elevator that the kitchen staff use to send food upstairs. There are several shelves breaking up the space, but that's...

Deadpool whips out a sword and hacks the shelves to little pieces. "Come on, Sixy Baby. Let's snuggle up."

Oh well. It's not as if you smell much less like road kill than he does at this point. "Fine."

He stares at you. "No getting handsy, okay? I like you, but this is not the time or the place."

"No way in–"

He lays a finger across your lips. "Shh. Just keep it in bottled up inside, Sixpence."

You shake your head. "No problem."

The pair of you cram in and push the button. The dumb-waiter whines, but it slowly creaks you upward.

You come out in a small, undecorated service room with a table in it but nothing else. Heading out leads you to a stretch of bland corridor. You can see a couple of security doors, one with a camera above it, the other with a card reader. There's also a standard wooden door, and a few safely abstract artworks to pretend to decoration.

> If you have a [Security Pass], you can swipe it in the card reader to turn to 75.
>
> If you have [Disguises], you can use those to get past the camera and turn to 295.
>
> Otherwise, you'll have to bash the wooden door down. Turn to 231.

190

Fantastic work! You haul the insectoid horror back to the boiler room and feed it into the purifying furnace. It swiftly burns, emitting thick clouds of green vapor that smell like forests. It makes your head spin, but you feel *incredible*, and barely chitinous at all.

Achievement: *Secret Hunter Seven* and achievement: *Check Out the Big Brain on Six*.

Split **+8** points between to your **MERC**, **MOUTH** and **FOCUS** in any combination you prefer, as the mutagenic fumes enhance the both of you.

Now go back to the lab corridor by turning to **295**.

191

Deadpool pushes the boss's door ajar and sticks his head in. "Hi!" he says brightly, then waves to you and goes in.

It's like stepping into the 1970s. The office is entirely decorated in oranges and browns with highlights of lime. The carpet is four inches deep, and the pattern makes you think of tricycle boys and murder-ghosts. The desk is vast and tasteless, and made of some slabby orange plastic. It's horrendous. Then you notice the dozen black-clad armed guards standing around. Your eardrums whimper. Behind the desk is a serious-looking middle aged man in a perfectly normal suit and a tasteful blue tie.

He stands up, and there's an alien-looking weapon in his hands. "Welcome." He sounds local, with an Ivy League polish. "I'm John Palmetto. They call me the Flail. I hope you've been having fun?"

Deadpool nods enthusiastically. "It's wonderful! I love the whole evil lair under Central Park thing. It's a real power move."

"Thank you. It was difficult and often frustrating, but we were pleased with how it came out. You should see the complex under Denver Airport, though."

"I've heard it's extensive."

"We have feeder branches all the way to Salt Lake City, Des Moines, and Albuquerque." He shudders. "Those servitors."

Deadpool blinks. "You're keeping shoggoths down there?"

"Ah." Palmetto sighs and lowers his head regretfully. "Time to die."

This is a boss fight.

If you have the [Razor-Ball] and want to… smooth this encounter, then by all means activate it. Observe as it zips around to drop every enemy in the room in an eye-blink, and turn to **274**.

If not, it's round one: roll one die and add your **FOCUS**. You win this round if the total is 5 or more. If you lose, Deadpool is shot by Palmetto's Chitauri gun, and you take **-3 MERC**.

Round two: roll three dice, and add both your **MERC** and your **FOCUS**. You win this round if the total is 17 or more. If you win, then Deadpool manages to take all the guards out of the fight, and you can add **+2** to your total in each subsequent round.

Round three: roll two dice, and add your **MERC**. You win this round if the total is 11 or more.

Round four: Roll two dice and add your **MERC**. You win this round if the total is 9 or more.

If you won at least three rounds, turn to **274**.

If not, turn to **64**.

192

Data in hand, Deadpool calls Weasel and puts him on speaker. "Hey, We–"

"I'm still alive!" you blurt in.

"And so very full of juicy, juicy organs," Weasel replies. "I never doubted you, Six. Not for an instant."

"I'm alive too," Deadpool says.

"Are you though, Wade? Really? Because it looks to me you're not even half-alive. You just roll from disaster to agonizing injury to despair, on and on, like a broken Furby that wakes you up at three in the morning muttering 'The time is now. The time is now. You always knew you'd know when it was time. That time is now.' Except the battery is really low, so the voice is really slow and drawn out, like spiders suddenly learned to talk, and–"

"No, I'm actually good."

"Oh. Cool. What's up?"

"I need you to turn some messy intel into a list of potential weapons dumps."

"Sure, send it over."

"Sending... now."

"What are you going to do with the list?" Weasel asks.

"Call someone who has the oomph to get rid of some of the sites, I guess."

"Spider-Man, then."

"Rot in hell, Weas." Deadpool hangs up.

A minute or two later, a plain-text list of sites comes through on the email. Deadpool looks at you. "So who are we calling?"

To call the army, turn to **253**.

To call the FBI, turn to **195**.

To call in the Avengers, turn to **242**.

To call Daredevil, turn to **291**.

To call Spider-Man, turn to **258**.

193

"We need to get a decent look around," you say. "We're just too hemmed in."

"On it," Deadpool says. He gathers himself and leaps fifteen feet into the air, flipping head over heels to land in a stylish three-point, knuckle-down crouch on top of a container. Then he leaps again, bouncing out of sight.

Thirty seconds later, you hear a faint noise, and look across the way to see him doing a hand-stand on top of a container crane. He flips back upright, then steps off the crane and plummets out of sight. There's a distant thud, and perhaps a groan. A minute later he comes back round the side of a container, limping slightly.

"Easy," he says. "There's a pack of thugs with guns across

the yard by some trucks, and they seem to have set up a nest of containers nearby. Where first?"

Take **+1 FOCUS**.

If you want to investigate the thugs, turn to **199**.

If you want to investigate the containers, turn to **8**.

194

There are eleven possibilities where at least one die is a 1 – roll a 1 and a 1, or a 1 and a 2, 2 and 1, 1 and 3, 3 and 1, etc. Only the first of those possibilities has the other die as a 1. So it's 1 in 11. Sorry. You only partially disable the lock.

"Great work, Mariachi," Deadpool says.

The left-hand cupboard opens, showing you a rough map of the complex. You make a note of the route to the command center. There are also three identical lockers in this cupboard, and you have time to open and potentially loot one of them.

To open locker one, turn to **226**.

To open locker two, turn to **248**.

To open locker three, turn to **84**.

195

Deadpool looks up the number for the FBI's New York field office and makes the call. After a moment, he groans. "Voicemail." He tries another number that doesn't answer, and a third number that just instantly hangs up on him. "Fine," he snarls. "We're going in person."

You head out and make your way to Federal Plaza. Deadpool has to leave his weapons with a startled door guard, but you get in. The FBI are on the 23rd floor, and you swan into the reception area. "Terrorists!" Deadpool bellows.

Take +1 {CHAOS}.

"Not us!" you yell, as everyone in sight leaps up and starts falling around like the crew on the bridge of a starship hit by enemy photon torpedoes. "Not here. Not right now. Don't panic!"

"Yeah." Deadpool calms down a little as a receptionist leads the pack heading over. "Do panic a bit, but not a whole heap."

In the mayhem you do get a chance to swipe a handy [FBI Badge] off the floor.

> If you want to try charm to calm everybody down, turn to **268**.
>
> If you want to try intimidation, turn to **153**.

196

The controller, whose name is Giselle Brown, spends several minutes going over all sorts of data outputs looking for discrepancies. Despite Deadpool's enthusiastic help, she eventually finds something odd.

"Look at this," she says, pointing to a screen showing a white box with a couple of white lines coming from it.

"That reminds me of an old friend," Deadpool says.

"This shouldn't be seeing any power draw, but it's pulling enough for a whole platform."

"Where is it?" you ask.

"It's a splice," she says. "There's nothing there. Does the name 'Second Family' mean anything to you? It's linked."

"No," Deadpool says. "But it will. This is perfect. Thanks, Giselle. Sorry for the fuss. I hope it works out with Robin."

Take +1 {SUSPICIOUS NAME} and the ACHIEVEMENT: *Mole Man.*

To follow up on your lead, turn to **86**.

Or, if you haven't already, try surface routes by turning to **43**.

Or, to try air routes, turn to **91**.

197

You watch in horror as Deadpool is fed noisily into the industrial wood-chipper. It takes a long time to grind him up, and somehow he keeps shrieking far longer than you'd expect. It is the sound of absolute torment. Everyone stops for a moment to watch in awe as his feet finally vanish with a gout of red gore. Then they all turn to look at you, and the guns come up.

ACHIEVEMENT: *You Had One Job.*

The end.

198

You approach the outhouse nervously, but there's no smell. In fact, as you crowd in with Deadpool, you discover the only thing inside is a bright metallic panel, occupying the far wall. The panel is engraved with a series of runic designs that glow with an electric-blue light. Each has a number attached.

This is a puzzle. The main body of the panel has runes attached to the numbers *63, 80, 99, 120,* and *143.* Below this are smaller, unlit runes next to the numbers *156, 168,* and *180.* You press one of these three smaller runes. It lights up, there's a dazzling flash, and you are... elsewhere.

If you pressed *156,* turn to **228**.

If you pressed *168,* turn to **62**.

If you pressed *180,* turn to **32**.

199

There are four trucks parked in a quiet corner of the port, and they're swarming with bald, over-muscled goons carrying machine-guns, and all wearing the same black sweaters. It's easy to spy on them, because one thing you're not short of is cover.

You watch for a few minutes, and see a constant parade of equally buff workers bringing crates from a battered-looking ship docked nearby. The workers know which vehicle they're headed for, and except for the occasional friendly nod, don't have any interaction with the truck guards.

One of the trucks is close to being full. If you go and get the car, you can try following it, or you can send Deadpool in to attack.

To try following the truck, turn to **207**.

To attack the thugs, turn to **21**.

200

The central office building is well signposted, and the harbormaster's office is easy enough to find. Deadpool breezes straight in there, past a secretary who squeaks and runs, and takes up a position in the center of the room. He points at the harbormaster. "You!"

The man looks confused. "Who the hell are you? What do you want? We're fully paid up. Wait, are the union boys causing trouble again?"

"Deadpool, Chimichangas, good for you, who cares."

"What?" says the harbormaster, more a protest than a question.

"What?" Deadpool asks back.

You decide to try to steer this conversation back onto something resembling the rails. "We're looking for some gun-runners," you say.

"Now just you loo*urkk*!" The harbormaster stops because suddenly Deadpool is standing there next to him with a sword pressed against the bottom of his nose.

"Don't make me cut off your nose," he says.

"You got it, buddy." The harbormaster finally looks scared. "*Those* gun-runners. They've got a boat down the end of Suez, but you can find most of them a bit further along Marsh by some trucks this morning."

"Thank you!" says Deadpool brightly, and pats the man's cheek.

Take **+1 MERC**.

If you want to investigate the ship, turn to **96**.

If you want to investigate the thugs, turn to **199**.

201

Hammerhead screams in fury as his soldiers stand down. He turns to the nearest one, a tall man with a leathery face, picks him up as easily as if he were a doll, and flings him straight through the window-frame to plummet screaming to his death. The others shuffle nervously back.

ACHIEVEMENT: *Learning to Fly.*

This is the second phase of the final boss fight.

Hammerhead sneers, discarding his rage like a used rag. "Youse always was a stupid dog, Wilson. Youse forgets, I *knows* ya. So I gots me this little toy in preparation." He holds up a small, vaguely gun-shaped thing that ends in a dish. "A neural jammer. Youse gonna like this one."

Make a **FOCUS** test. Roll one die and add your **FOCUS**. If you brought along a [Cheery Log] for comfort, add **+2** to your total.

10 or more: Nothing seems to happen. Hammerhead curses and crushes the device to powder in his paw-like hand. Turn immediately to **19**.

9 or less: Deadpool writhes in horrified pain. Set your **MERC**, **MOUTH**, and **FOCUS** to 1, and then reduce one of them down to 0.

> If you want to keep trying to fight with Deadpool crippled, turn to **19**.

> To surrender now, turn to **30**.

202

In one corner, you notice a box made of gleaming metal. It looks well cared-for. You pick your way over to it. To your surprise, it opens easily. Inside, nestled on a velvet cushion, is a wicked looking [Razor-Ball], an impossibly shiny metal sphere with a large, menacing razorblade spike sticking out the front. It's about palm-sized – well, palm-sized for a taller man, anyway. It looks truly horrible. You might like to take it with you.

ACHIEVEMENT: *Secret Hunter Two*. Congratulations! There's nothing for it now but to return to **282**.

203

The ancient hut might once have been a little dwelling. The weedy thicket out front might be the devolution of a garden, and something like a window seems to glint through the thick creepers. It's oppressive, and the closer you get, the more unwelcome you feel.

"This is like my old barracks," Deadpool says. "I wonder if anyone's home."

No one has been home for decades. "I hope not."

"Come on, this place lies." He pushes the mossy screen door open, and steps in.

You follow, walking into a pulsing psychic wave of hatred and aggression. The room is empty, apart from a carpet of unidentifiable debris, but it *wants* to kill you.

Then the debris stirs, swirls, flows together into something like a man but far too wide, with black voids where its eyes should be. It lumbers straight for Deadpool.

This is a hard fight.

Round one: roll two dice and add your **FOCUS**. If the total is at least 12, you win the first round.

Round two: roll two dice and add your **FOCUS**. If the total is at least 12, you win the second round.

This bizarre thing is too slow to be really dangerous to Deadpool, but if you won both rounds, he manages to break the thing down quickly, so take **+1 MERC** and **+1 FOCUS**.

Outside, nearer the front of the compound, you see a couple of new structures.

If you have not done so already, try the once-red shed by turning to **228**.

To examine the oddly clean outhouse, turn to **198**.

204

The locker creaks... and opens!

Take **+1** {PUZZLER}.

Inside the locker is a complex alien [Time Grenade]. If you take it, you can detonate it later to win two rounds of any one fight.

You hear a hiss, and look up. Uh-oh. Gas? You try to hold your breath, but the world goes fuzzy, and you slump to the ground. Turn to **33**.

205

This room holds several battered tables and a series of vending machines loaded with forty-two varieties of sweet and salty snacks. Deadpool heads straight over to them.

"Hey, Six, my oldest and dearest friend. Do you have a bunch of change?"

"Oh, I never bring my wallet on operations," you say. Not after yesterday.

"Weirdo." He leaps into the air, and kicks the nearest vending machine hard, at the top of its frame. It wobbles back and forward worryingly.

Make a senseless violence test. Roll one die, and add your **MERC** to it.

Total of 5 or more: A cascade of snacks pours out. Mmm, snacks. Take **+1 MERC**.

4 or less: The machine falls over, shorting the whole bank. No snacks.

To go back to the corridor, turn to **24**.

To head past the corridor, turn to **217**.

206

You leave the stunned party and walk through into another large room, this one set up as a temporary art gallery for the auction later.

The people in here are no less wealthy, but they're less obviously ostentatious about it. Most are browsing the art, which appears to be a selection of marble sculptures, flat pieces carved in bas-relief.

Several servers and assistants are working the room, in black hotel uniforms with gold-trim, and there's a larger and much fancier buffet of foods and drinks along one wall. At the back of the room, a heavy door with a fancy-looking card reader is partly hidden behind two armed guards and a partially drawn gold velvet curtain.

"If we had a distraction, I could lift a card," Deadpool says. "Can you do it?"

You think of the spluttering Mafia don in the previous room. Onwards seems the better option. "Sure."

To start a food fight, turn to **280**.

To smash some art, turn to **257**.

To set fire to the room, turn to **246**.

To have Deadpool attack the door guards, turn to **99**.

207

You hurry back out of the dock to where Deadpool parked his ludicrous car, and you both pile back in. The truck hasn't left yet – it would have had to come past you. It's a couple more minutes before you hear it rumbling towards the gates. Deadpool guns the engine and once the truck leaves, you follow.

Ideally, you would have used a less conspicuous vehicle than a bright yellow blob that looks like someone squashed a fly and put wheels on the corpse. The truck immediately speeds off, and turns off down a side-road into an industrial area.

You follow. The car is painfully slow, and there are lots of trucks in this area, but you know which one you're after. Maybe.

It's time for a (humiliatingly low-speed) chase minigame!

Round 1: test your **FOCUS** (roll one die, and add your **FOCUS**.) Your goal is 5 or more. If you succeed, subtract 1 from the goal. If you fail, add 1 to it.

Round 2: test your **FOCUS** again, with the new goal. Again, if you succeed, subtract 1 from the goal, and if you fail, add 1 to it.

Round 3: test your **FOCUS** one last time, with the freshly revised goal.

Did you succeed in at least two rounds?

    Yes: turn to **36**.

    No: turn to **93**.

208

A carp-laden door opens, and a woman in cleaner's overalls comes out of a bedroom. Her eyes widen.

"*Por favor, chica,*" Deadpool says. "*Silencio.* If you scream, lots of people die. You too, maybe. Do you care if some rich white *calabazas* lose some money?" She shakes her head and re-enters the room, and you go into the white room.

Make a persuasion test. Roll one die, and add both your **MERC** and your **MOUTH** to the total.

9 or more: You climb down the ladder to **83**.

8 or less: You hear an alarm as you enter. Turn to **129**.

209

There's nothing to particularly distinguish the Folklore building from the rest of the campus. It doesn't look sinister, it's not tucked away in a distant corner, and vines utterly fail to smother it in an attempt to hide their shame. There's a lesson in that somewhere.

The classrooms, for example. A list on the wall puts Professor Hope on the ground floor, off to the left of the small, peaceful lobby. You follow the corridor, which leads round towards the back of the building. It's very deliberately old academic – dark wooden paneling, tile floors, off-white ceiling, occasional pieces of artwork. Perfectly innocuous. Nice, even.

Have you attracted notice?

Make a security test. Roll one die, add your **FOCUS**, and subtract your {**GUARDS, GUARDS**} rating, if any.

Total of 5 or more: turn to **80**.

4 or less: turn to **125**.

210

Talon Minor is surprisingly fast, but you manage to keep them in sight as they slip into a high-end department store.

An office worker in a department store. Ouch. It's not peak shopping hours, but the store is still busy.

Make a search test. Roll one die and add your **FOCUS** to it.

> 6 or more: turn to **66**.
>
> 5 or less: you do follow someone, but it's not the right someone. Turn to **216**.

211

Hammerhead collapses, Deadpool's thighs clamped around his neck, choking him out.

How much damage did you do to Hammerhead's plans? Add up your {CASH DOWN}, {WEAPONS DOWN}, and {NAMES DOWN}, if any. What's the total?

> If it's 5 or less, or your {CHAOS} is 16 or more (or both!), turn to **22**.
>
> If it's 6 or more, turn to **106**.
>
> Alternatively, if your {DISCORD} is 6 or more and you're fed up of Deadpool and want to stab him in the back – you villain, you! – instead turn to **42**.

212

Warbird, whose real name is Ava'Dara Naganandini, was affiliated to the X-Men as a member of Jean Gray's School for Higher Learning. She is not the odd one out. Sorry. Go back to **216**.

213

You shake your head. This is all just way too much. "I'm sorry, I can't."

Deadpool slumps, looking profoundly depressed. "I'm not going to force you to help. I'm trying to get better about that, and anyway, you're not blind. But I really do need your help. You're not like the rest of these… people."

He waves an arm to indicate the small park, taking in all the other people around you who are, unusually, not there. It's just the two of you. "You and I both know you're special. You've got a real person watching over your shoulder. If you don't help, I'm just not going to be able to continue, and I don't know what will happen then. I'll probably wind up back in some comic. That would really be a waste of this book, don't you think?"

"I'm not following you," you say.

"But you could, Sixter. You could if you wanted to. *Please?*"

His little speech may have been incoherent, but it was strangely moving. Or maybe that's just your breakfast settling. Either way, you consider it again.

"Okay, I'll help." Turn to **35**.

"I just can't." Turn to **40**.

214

A concentrated blast of machine-gun fire tears a hole in Deadpool's pelvis. *Ouchy.* He falls, and guards surround him, smashing his head with their clubs. Then the Professor steps up and empties a very large jar of acid on the remains, which start dissolving. You make a noise. One of the guards looks up at you, and everything goes black. Just imagine. Deadpool, killed by tetchy university staff. Truly, this is the darkest timeline.

ACHIEVEMENT: *Dying of Embarrassment.*

The end.

215

This is a store room, all right. Cramped, lots of wooden shelving, all sorts of office and cleaning supplies, a bucket and mop behind the door, a suspiciously gleaming metal panel at the back looking completely out of place against the white plasterboard...

Huh. You head over to the panel, and give it an experimental prod. It clatters to the floor, revealing a complex electronic circuit board and, on a small ledge beneath it, a small vial of [Sparkling Powder] that you could take.

To tackle the circuit board puzzle, turn to **163**.

To go back to the corridor, turn to **295**.

216

Deadpool's safe-house is one of several dozen five-by-fifteen storage units within a warren of reeking corridors that lurk within a cheap warehouse. There's just a stained, rat-gnawed office chair in there, plus a stack of old pizza boxes. He graciously lets you have the chair, as if leptospirosis is a treat rather than a potentially fatal disease.

If your {OUT OF TIME} is 8 or more, you're, uh, out of time – for preparations, that is. Go to **46** right now.

If not, Deadpool looks up at you from his greasy cockroach-ridden pizza throne. "Okay, Six. What should we tackle?"

To try sabotaging the network's funding, turn to **178**.

To try warning the bad guys on the hit list, turn to **115**.

To try reducing the number of weapon caches, turn to **113**.

To gather resources of your own, turn to **119**.

217

The sturdy door at the end of the service corridor is unlocked. You go through into a shorter stretch of corridor, this one lightly carpeted.

"Nice carpet," Deadpool says. "Looks like it belongs to a bottom-feeding PI with alcoholism and near-terminal stubbornness, who's about to get their life turned over by a pretty face with a sad story."

"How does it end?"

"Badly, of course. Like all carpets. It's not surprising there's no one about. Who'd want to walk over something this sad?"

There are a couple of doors, ones with real signs this time.

If you want to try *Control*, turn to **241**.

If you want to try *Office*, turn to **245**.

218

You turn to the pilot. "Have you seen any suspicious activity in the last week, Mr. Davies?"

He thinks for a moment. "Actually, I have seen some shadowy looking birds coming into Queens a few times recently. We could go look round there?"

"Sure," you say, managing not to shrug. "Let's try it."

Some time later, you're flying north over a run-down looking light industrial district when the pilot points off to one side at a black helicopter. "There. That's one of them. It doesn't have any numbers, which is seriously dumb if you're trying to keep a low profile. I can try following it, but I think I know where it took off from."

Deadpool watches you expectantly.

To approach the black helicopter, turn to **29**.

To examine the building it left, turn to **79**.

219

You climb down the ladder into the middle of a circular white room. A ring of red lights is flashing unpleasantly in the ceiling. Three curved metal doors are set into the wall, spaced evenly. As you come down, there's a faint grinding and the wall begins to spin, faster and faster, the doors blurring into invisibility. Then it slams to a stop with an audible *thunk!*

It's time for a progress minigame!

First, let's see how you're doing. If your {DRAGONFIRE} is 8 or more, take +1 {DISCORD}, -1 MERC, and -2 MOUTH, and skulk on over to **24** in humiliation.

Now, make a luck test. Roll one die, adding 1 if your {DRAGONFIRE} is 5 or more.

> If you get 6 or more: A small lightning bolt crackles out of a dome in the ceiling and zaps both of you. Take -1 FOCUS and +1 {DRAGONFIRE} and re-start this entry.
>
> If you get 3 or less: A door opens onto a corridor. Turn to entry **24**.

Otherwise (ie, on a 4 or 5), a door opens to admit a small group of guards, leading to a moderate fight.

Round one: roll two dice and add your MERC. If the total is at least 10, you win the first round.

Round two: roll two dice and add your MERC. If the total is at least 10, you win the second round.

Take -1 MERC for each round you lost. Now the wall starts moving again. Take +1 {DRAGONFIRE} and restart this entry from the very beginning.

Maybe half of the customers are still here, ready to fight. Unfortunately, it looks like they're the tough portion. You can see pieces of body armor under some jackets, and several of the men bring out machine-guns. At some signal you can't make out, they open up. The noise is deafening. Scrunched up down by the jukebox, you wrap your arms around your head and hope. Then there is only gunfire, punctuated occasionally by a wild scream. It seems to go on for hours, but it really can only have been a few seconds. You just hope that Deadpool is enjoying himself.

This is a moderate fight.

Round one: roll two dice and add your **MERC**. If the total is at least 10, you win the first round.

Round two: roll two dice and add your **MERC**. If the total is at least 10, you win the second round.

If you won both rounds, turn to **263**.

If not, turn to entry **98**.

221

You follow the corridor ahead to another metal door. This one isn't locked, and you go through into a laboratory that looks like a high-tech version of one of Dr Frankenstein's lairs. There's a whole range of machines of uncertain purpose, from the boxy to the abstract. Several of them are going *ping!* You also see complicated chains of chemistry apparatuses feeding into one another, a bristling array of microscopes and viewers, too many tools to mention, and, dominating the center of the room, a big metal table with obvious blood-gutters.

"I think someone is over*com*pensating," Deadpool trills. "Ooh, look at the huge lab I have. So impressive. So... delightful."

"All the better to augment you with, my dear?" you suggest.

Deadpool blinks. "If you want to augment me, Number Six, you have to buy me dinner first."

There's nothing obviously useful in here.

> To exit through the door on the left side of the lab, turn to **292**.
>
> To retrace your steps and try the left-hand corridor, turn to **273**.

222

You go through the door on the left into a large, luxuriously carpeted conference room with a big, expensive looking oak table surrounded by unusually comfy-looking work chairs. Whereas the corridor was all gray, this room is more tastefully decorated in earth tones.

There are a few folders on the table. If you have a {WET} score of 1 or more, they're already ruined to the point of illegibility, alas. If not, you find an interestingly detailed sketch of a corporate building: take +1 {ART HINT}.

Heading on through the conference room leads you to a small water cooler area, complete with a breakfast nook and a pair of doors leading to a pair of bathrooms, as well as a frosted glass door to the main office.

To check the breakfast nook, turn to **294**.

To use the bathroom, turn to **90**.

To finally visit the boss, turn to **191**.

223

"I've got some leads on things we might be able to use," Deadpool says. "You know how it is, though – someone knows someone who knows a man with a flock of crows that carry whispers from across the city and they've told him about a really shiny bauble in the long grass by the Battery, but there's a rogue Chihuahua closing on the location and the dog-catcher doesn't appear to be in place yet, and... Well. Tuesdays, basically."

"Great," you say, cautiously. "So what's available?"

Take +1 {RESOURCEFUL}.

Make an availability test. Roll a die. If you have a

[Sparkling Icosahedron], you may destroy it to re-roll. As a final option, you may take +2 {OUT OF TIME} to pick a specific result instead of rolling.

1: "Weapons." Turn to **150**.

2: "Tricks." Turn to **154**.

3: "Some much needed R&R, Six." Turn to **140**.

4: "Space to breathe." Turn to **39**

5: "Bribe money." Turn to **239**.

6: "Help." Turn to **18**.

224

Leaving the fetid ritual chamber behind, you press on. There's a network of tunnels, but at each junction, only one passage glows with phosphorescence, and since you trust us now (right?), you take that path.

After about twenty increasingly claustrophobic minutes, the walls start getting rougher and less regular. The topography of this area seems odd. You come to spots ahead too quickly, or too slowly. The ceiling descends until you have to bend in places, whilst in others it soars above you like the roof of a cathedral.

Finally, you arrive at a junction with two phosphorescent ways forward, one jaggedly rough, one weirdly smooth. Where the ways diverge, you find a [Crank-Handle] from some old well, which you may take.

To take the jagged way, turn to **45**.

To take the glassy way, turn to **120**.

225

Wow, you *have* been busy! Good work. Disruption synergizes, so take an extra +1 to {CASH DOWN}, {NAMES DOWN}, {WEAPONS DOWN}, and {RESOURCEFUL}. Hammerhead won't know what hit him, we're sure. ACHIEVEMENT: *One With Everything*.

If you *also* have at least 1 in each of {TOOLED UP}, {ZANY}, {FEELING GOOD}, {AWARE}, and {FLUSH}, award yourself +1 MERC, MOUTH, and FOCUS, -1 to {CHAOS}, the ACHIEVEMENT: *My Best Me*, and turn to entry 3.

Otherwise, press on to 243.

226

You open the first locker. You can already hear boots approaching faintly. Inside is a [USB Key]. You know it's a key because it has *Pass Key* written on it in silver Sharpie. You may take it if you like, but remember you can have five items maximum.

Now you need to get moving before someone actually sane and threatening finds you.

To head to the command suite, turn to 232.

To head to the storage area, turn to 282.

227

"Great," Deadpool says, grabbing a marker and scribbling an address label. "Teenage Negasonic Warhead will know *exactly* how to use three free crates of Chitauri Guns. Better mark it 'Private and Confidential' so Colossus doesn't poke around. There."

She will indeed.

Take **-2 {CHAOS}** – paid to you now, courtesy of the near future.

If you go on to the command suite, turn to entry **232**.

If you stay in Shipping, turn to **255**, but don't come back here – the reduction in {CHAOS} can only happen once.

228

You're in front of a shed door that was once red. Now, however, it is unwholesomely spongy, and when you push on it, it doesn't so much open as slough away. The interior is like some alien environment, a dank grotto of fungal blooms and growths like none you've ever seen before. Some of them are tall and slender, a few even glowing with faint greens and blues, while others resemble craters, or dripping mouths, or pustulent rocks.

You're absolutely certain that you can hear something breathing.

Deadpool walks in a few steps, says "Nope," turns around and heads back out.

You can't disagree.

Take +1 {SPORE-SEEDED}.

To go to the warehouse you saw earlier, turn to **77**.

There's also a decrepit trailer-office visible further in. To try that, turn to **168**.

229

The crowd surges forward. There are lots of guns out, but the guys further back don't have a shot, so they're bringing out big knives, chunks of pipe, billy clubs, and in one case, an honest-to-goodness half-brick. You swiftly get out the way as Deadpool wades in, and take shelter down beside a heavy-looking old jukebox.

Almost immediately, Deadpool is surrounded. There's a flurry of shots and thumps, and a number of groans and curses. In a momentary lull, through your ringing ears, you hear what sounds like a trapdoor thudding closed behind the bar. Deadpool says something. Several goons yell incoherently, and you think you hear one actually growl like a bear. The crowd surges, and the fight resumes.

This is a simple fight.

Round one: roll two dice and add your **MOUTH**. If the total is at least 8, you win the first round.

Round two: roll two dice and add your **MERC**. If the total is at least 8, you win the second round.

If you won both rounds, turn to **220**; otherwise turn to **98**.

230

The big man growls in the back of his throat and shakes his head, dismissing Deadpool from his mind. Deadpool tries a couple more insults, then clambers up onto the feed belt, drawing a sword. The boss eyes him as the belt brings him closer, then crouches in a fighter's stance, hands wide and low. It strikes you that a conveyor belt feeding swiftly into a huge shredder is a really dumb place for a fight.

If you want Deadpool to try to wrestle the boss off the conveyor, make a wrestling test. Roll one die, and add your **MERC** to it.

On a score of 8 or more, the fight moves down – turn to **108**.

Otherwise, turn to **183**.

231

Deadpool takes a run-up and charges the wooden door, leaping into a kick at the last moment. There's a loud crash.

You would've called it deafening before – oh, for the good old days when you still had eardrums.

Take **+1 {WARNED}**.

Make a timing test. Roll one die and add your **FOCUS**.

On a score of 8 or more: turn to **75**.

7 or less: turn to **132**.

232

You carefully pick your way through the complex. Deadpool seems remarkably focused and professional, keeping quiet and low, avoiding guards. Sure, he's playing hopscotch on the floor tiles as you go, but you can't have everything.

The way into the command suites proves to be a pleasant reception lobby. It's tastefully furnished, if a bit heavy on the chrome and white leather, and several pleasant pastoral artworks hang on the walls. The lobby is slightly spoiled by all the red flashing alert lights everywhere, which provide the only illumination. There's a reception desk, but there's no one behind it, and the wooden door leading on into the suites is locked.

Deadpool looks around. "I like it. Reminds me of being born."

You stare at him. "You remember that?"

"No, but I'm certain there were lots of red flashing lights. That's normal for births."

"It really isn't."

"I was born in *Canada*, Sixxon. Speaking of which, how

about we try to trick our way inside? That's always been a great standby for me."

If you have an [Alien Gun] and want to use it, turn to **136**.

To try Deadpool's trick, turn to **103**.

To assault the door, turn to **186**.

233

Apparently, Dr Lundt is primarily engaged in mathematics. The walls are covered with chalk boards, which are in turn filled of cramped equations and other notations. You're not sure whether they're one piece, or a whole swathe of different calculations. There's a desk in here, and a window looking out onto the street, but there's no one in here. Deadpool picks up a piece of chalk, and starts altering important details here and there. How do you back up a chalk board anyway? Oh well.

The desk is boring, apart from a small twisted pyramid of spiky metal. If you want the [Caltrop], you may take it. It can be used once to give yourself a **+2** to die rolls in every round of any one fight.

Then there's a flash of actinic blue, a pop of displaced air, and a portly man appears. His eyes widen, there's another flash, and he's gone again with another pop.

Take **+1 {WARNED}**.

Now, to return to the corridor, turn to **295**.

To use the door directly to Dr Smythe's lab, turn to **12**.

234

Air vents? Really? Do you live on a Hollywood action movie set or something? We suppose next you'll be climbing through some magically sturdy person-sized ducts that just happen to catacomb the ceiling space. We *did* say the door was the only break in the solid metal walls. So, you go through into a concrete corridor, done out in fallout shelter chic. Now you're at a corner.

To go straight ahead, turn to **221**.

To head left, turn to **273**.

235

The door to Records leads you, via a stretch of corridor, to a few rough stone steps and a heavy wooden door. The door is open.

"That's handy, Hexie," Deadpool mutters as you follow him through into the Academy's former wine cellars. They must have kept an insane amount of wine down here. That naughty Emma Frost. Now it's a chaotic hubbub of boxes, files, and suited minions. The room is packed with material, all of it being funneled to a high conveyor belt leading to an enormous industrial-sized wood-chipper.

The boss of this operation is standing astride the conveyor belt near the shredder's mouth. You can tell he's the boss, because he's about seven feet tall, with lavender skin, and his suit is exquisite. Besides, everyone else is clearly terrified of him. He's frantically pitching boxes into the maw – documents, drives, laptops, all sorts. Maybe this isn't about your infiltration after all. A couple of the suit-wearing minions have looked round to see you, but they don't seem to care.

If you want to attack the minions, turn to **128**.

If you want to ignore them and head deeper, turn to **298**.

236

The vault is stacked to the gunnels with bricks of bank notes. The good news is that money can be used to buy goods and services. The bad news is that it is very, very bulky, and you don't have a fleet of armored trucks to carry it away with. Deadpool is just pawing gently at the bricks. He might even be weeping.

If you want to steal as much money as you can carry, take **+1 {CASH DOWN}**, **+1 {FLUSH}**, and **+1 {OUT OF TIME}**.

If instead you want to go outside and encourage other folks to help steal the money too, take **+2 {CASH DOWN}**, **+1 {FLUSH}**, **+1 {OUT OF TIME}** and **+3 {CHAOS}**.

If, however, you want to burn it all, that's quick and thorough. Take **+3 {CASH DOWN}**.

Afterward, head back to the safe-house and turn to **216**.

237

Atlantic City is basically one long, over-developed beach front. Everything in sight seems finely tuned to extract wealth from tourists with as small an overhead as possible. The casinos might not be the pinnacle of this ecosystem, for there may be crueler predators lurking behind the glittering lights or under the extensive boardwalks, but they're certainly the most prominent. The Golden Table Casino is just a depressing apartment tower with an ugly sign. Deadpool looks at it and sighs happily. "I love Jersey."

"You do?"

"It just makes me feel at home, you know?" You consider that. There are definitely parallels.

Against all reason, there's a concierge at a complimentary parking stand out the front. He looks startled when you pull up, and appalled when Deadpool flips him the keys.

The casino's lobby looks like the interior of a cheap hotel that's been dying for thirty years. The place where you buy casino chips is all modern and inviting, and surrounded by sparkling ATMs, but everything else is shabby at best. There's a seedy bar off to one side, and a maze of slot machines which eventually gives way to gaming tables. A signboard in the middle of the floor points off to a charity auction in the Timberline Suite.

To check the bar, turn to **270**.

To try the slots, turn to **164**.

To investigate the auction, turn to **262**.

Driving along in the weakly car-like machine, Deadpool calls Weasel and sets him on speakerphone.

"Wade, buddy! How's the limpet?"

"Patelliform, thanks. Remind me not to hire one of these cars again."

"Don't hire one of those cars again, you ludicrous turnip."

"Thanks, Weas."

"Any time. Was there anything else?"

"Probably." Deadpool thinks for a moment. "Hammer-head."

"The mobster?"

"Yeah."

"What about him?"

"What you got on his personnel at the moment? I've got to go kick his butt, and he's loaded to the teeth with stolen Chitauri guns. He's in the Meteorite Building."

"You're gonna die, and so will that sad-faced Muppet you're dangling around like a safety plushie. There's no chance. He's going to completely destroy you both and use your pulped organs to help feed up his pet steroid casualties. Hey, he might keep you regenerating and being harvested for an endless supply of long pork steaks. This is the end, buddy. Can I have your posters?"

"No. Is that all you've got?"

"Of course not."

He reels off a bunch of information that doesn't mean all

that much to you, but Deadpool nods as if it's useful. After some more banter, he hangs up.

Take +1 {ORG SEC} and +1 {OUT OF TIME}.

If you are carrying [Intel], take an extra +1 {ORG SEC} and discard the [Intel].

If you have {NO (SUB)WAY} of 1, take an extra +1 {OUT OF TIME} for the congestion.

Now, to research the network's structure, turn to **70**.

To get to the safe-house, turn to **216**.

239

Deadpool takes you into Manhattan, to a cheap-looking bank he claims is his regular branch. When he walks in, the staff definitely get wary, but no one screams for help or anything. Huh. They probably *do* know him.

Take +1 {OUT OF TIME}.

"How do you want me to work this, Six?"

"Work what?"

"Getting some money out."

You blink. "Normally?"

Deadpool shakes his head. "Too predictable."

Right. Fine.

If you say, "Be nice," turn to **151**.

If you say, "Be weird," turn to **172**.

240

The bar's name, The Hollow, left you vaguely optimistic about somewhere cosy and nook-like. Unfortunately, it's gone full out for the "empty, depressing void" interpretation. It's a small corner bar that's clearly been looking rough since the 70s, the kind of dive that never gets any passing traffic because no one who isn't used to it would ever step inside voluntarily. It must be crooked, because in the modern property market, there's no way it could survive, even out here.

If you want to walk in like customers, turn to **130**.

If you want to crash in like enemies, turn to **289**.

241

"I didn't do this. I'm certain. Fairly certain. I probably didn't do this. I hope it wasn't me. Was it me?"

"No. It wasn't you," you confirm. It's easy to see why Deadpool's confused, though. This might have been a vibrant operations center packed with computer equipment earlier, but now it's a mess of charred circuitry and melted plastic. No corpse pile, which makes a nice change.

There is nothing of use or interest here, unless you want to craft yourself a neo-primitivist necklace out of wire and shattered components. (No, it's not an item, and doesn't go in your inventory. If you want to pretend you're decked out like last century's apocalypse, don't let us stop you. You do you.)

A door at the back of the room leads on to the records office.

If you want to go to Records, turn to **235**.

If you want to go back to the corridor and into the office, turn to **245**.

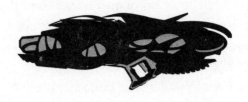

242

Deadpool winces, but he calls a number in his speed-dial list, and puts it on speakerphone.

It's answered quickly. "Hello, Wade," says a wearily suspicious voice with a thick Russian accent. "What is it now? Beavers again?"

"What? No," Deadpool says. "The beavers are Michigan's problem now. It's Hammerhead. He's got a network of Chitauri gun caches spread across the country and he's about to unleash them in an orgy of death."

"Chit… This is dreadful! A disaster…" There's a long pause. "And *you* just happen to know, and are coming to *us* for help? I do not think so."

"But it's true," Deadpool whines.

"Like the mermaids ambushing the sea cruise, or the Senator stuck in the mystical toilet in Arby's? No, Wade. Enough lies."

Make a persuasion test. Roll one die, and add your **MOUTH** and your {CHAOS}.

If your total is 12 or more, Colossus puts some of the recent madness together, and agrees to help – something he's very good at. Take **+3** {WEAPONS DOWN} and **-1** {OUT OF TIME}.

If the total is 11 or less, Colossus reluctantly agrees to at least look at the list. Take **+1** {WEAPONS DOWN}.

Now turn to **216**.

243

The Meteorite Building. It's a stylish name with reassuringly sinister undertones. Disappointingly, it's just a bland office building, four floors tall, broadly identical to tens of thousands of others of New York eyesores. From the outside, you can see the lobby is swarming with people wearing brightly-colored three-piece suits, most of them sapphire blue. There are a lot of big guns on display.

We need to see how much noise you've made on your way here. What's your current {CHAOS} rating?

5 or less: set {WARNED} to 1.

6-10: set {WARNED} to 2.

11-15: set {WARNED} to 3.

16 or more: set {WARNED} to 4 and take the ACHIEVEMENT: *Chaos Puppy*.

Next, you might have some options on how to progress.

If you have {GUTSY} of 1 or more, you may make a daring entrance by turning to **11**.

If you have {DARK SECRET} of 1 or more, you may do something mind-rending by turning to **133**.

If you have an [Alien Weapon], you may blast your way in savagely by turning to **284**.

If you have {ART HINTS} of 2 or more, you may use a semi-secret staff door by turning to **135**.

If none of those options are available – or you're just in a violent mood – you can launch a frontal attack on the lobby, which even from outside looks very heavily guarded. To go on the offensive, check your {WARNED}.

If it's 1, turn to **95**.

If it's 2 or more, turn to **53**.

244

Hammerhead looks at the carnage where his soldiers used to be, clapping slowly. "The mighty Deadpool, slaughterer of helpless chumps. Feelin' good abouts yaself, Wilson?"

"You killed them, Hammerhead. I was just the weapon."

"Whatever gets ya through the night, pal."

"Your elite soldiers are always psychos, Joeboy. I'm doing the world a favor. And there's still one more piece of trash to take out."

Hammerhead sneers. "Youse always was a stupid dog, Wilson. Youse forgets, I *knows* ya. So I gots me this little toy in preparation." He holds up a small, vaguely gun-shaped thing that ends in a dish. "A neural jammer. Youse gonna like this one."

This is the second phase of the final boss fight.

Make a **FOCUS** test. Roll one die and add your **FOCUS**. If you brought along a [Cheery Log] for comfort, add **+2** to your total.

> 10 or more: Nothing seems to happen. Hammerhead curses and crushes the device to powder in his paw-like hand. Turn immediately to **19**.
>
> 9 or less: Deadpool writhes in horrified pain. Set your **MERC**, **MOUTH**, and **FOCUS** to 1, and then reduce one of them down to 0.
>
> If you want to keep trying to fight, turn to **19**.
>
> To surrender now, turn to **30**.

245

You walk into a modestly apportioned, open-plan office. It's not quite a cubicle farm, but it's not exactly a nurturing environment either. There's got to be a dozen or more desks, but every drawer is open, every box empty, and there isn't a scrap of paper to be found. A door at the back of the room leads on to the records office.

"We finally found it, Sixington. It's real. The paperless office! You know what this means, right?"

"Someone's hiding data?"

"It means a truly profitable career on the conference circuit, my friend. All those executives hunting for the Grail. We've seen it. We're set for life."

"What about those?" You point at some large framed photographs of a city business district.

Deadpool sags in despair. "Reed's floppy pool noodles. We were *that* close."

Take **+1 {ART HINT}**.

If you want to go to Records, turn to **235**.

If you want to go back to the corridor and into the control room, turn to **241**.

246

Deadpool hands you a little plastic lighter in a cheerful cover, then moves back. You go and stand next to the buffet, then surreptitiously light the cloth. As it begins to catch, you go to some nearby gold drapes, and set them alight too. Then you turn away, and walk towards the center of the room. No one protests. A few moments later, you hear a gasp. You look round to see the drape start truly blazing, and the buffet beginning to go up. There's a scream, then heavy sprinklers come on, and everyone is suddenly running for the door shrieking. The guards are out in the room, looking at each other, and don't notice Deadpool pass behind them. He nods to you.

Take **+1 FOCUS** and **+1 {CHAOS}**, and the ACHIEVEMENT: *They Love Me In That Buffet.*

You have a clear moment. Deadpool swipes the card, and the door makes a clicking sound. There's a big red button next to the door as well though.

If you tug on the door, turn to **160**.

If you push the button, turn to **55**.

247

The remaining guards – eleven of them now – exchange grim looks, then close in on Deadpool, attempting to work as a unified pack.

This is a moderate fight.

Round one: roll two dice and add your **MERC**. If the total is at least 10, you win the first round.

Round two: roll two dice and add your **MOUTH**. If the total is at least 10, you win the second round.

Round three: roll two dice and add your **MERC**. If the total is at least 9, you win the third round.

If you won at least two rounds, turn to **124**.

If you lost at least two rounds, turn to **33**.

248

You open the second locker. You can already hear boots approaching faintly. Inside is an intriguing [Encrypted File]. It might be important. Who encrypts their shopping? You may take the file if you like. Remember you can only carry five items maximum.

Now you need to get moving before someone actually sane and threatening finds you.

To head to the command suite, turn to **232**.

To head to the storage area, turn to **282**.

249

You enter the elevator. It only has one other button apart from the first floor, so you press it.

Make a luck test. Roll one die.

1-3: turn to entry **139**.

4-6: turn to entry **132**.

250

The controller hurries over towards the two of you, looking nervous but resolute. She's a stern-faced woman in her fifties, clearly no one to be trifled with.

Deadpool goes to meet her. "I'm sorry about all this,"

he tells her. "Terrorists are using the subway to smuggle shipments of alien weapons. We need your help to search the network for unscheduled movements or out of place stops, so we can work out where they are." She doesn't look convinced. "Please?"

In the background, you notice a greasy little guy stand up. He shoots you a truly poisonous look, types something on his keyboard, then hurries out of the room.

Test your **FOCUS** – roll one die, and add your **FOCUS** to it. What's the total?

> 4 or more: turn to **196**.
> 3 or less: turn to **277**.

251

There's no need to ruin this poor guy's day. "We can wait for your paying clients and sit in the back," you tell him.

"There's room," he replies cautiously, and sags in relief as Deadpool shrugs and then nods.

Fortunately it's not long until the businessmen arrive. They are very polite about your presence, and seem intrigued. You're just lifting off, headset on, when Deadpool launches into a long, confusing, and highly implausible story about how he spent three years as a gangster sumo wrestler.

Take **+1 MOUTH**.

A few minutes later, Deadpool is describing one particular piece of gunkanmaki sushi, and one of the businessmen is so moved as to be on the verge of tears. One of his companions is busily filming the whole thing on his cellphone. The pilot is shaking his head, but the helicopter is keeping him busy. Apparently it's up to you to get things back on track.

If you want to hunt for possibly suspicious aircraft, turn to **185**.

If you want to ask the pilot if he's seen anything odd, turn to **218**.

252

You turn to Deadpool. "Back me up." You've seen tech guru types on television. You stride straight at the young woman, keeping your face blank. She smiles at you, her eyes as emotionless as the void. "Arterton," you snap. "Dominion."

Take **+1 MOUTH**.

She glances at her clipboard. Not a single muscle so much as twitches out of place. "I'm sor–"

"Stop." You sneer, and jerk your head towards Deadpool. "That is my bodyguard. Are you actually stupid enough to imagine I ever appear on a *list*?"

"Of course," the woman says, completely unruffled. Whatever she earns, she's underpaid. "Would you–"

"No," you snap, and stride on past.

Make an arrogance test. Roll one die, and add your **MOUTH** to it.

Total 5 or more: turn to **4**.

4 or less: turn to **13**.

253

Deadpool shrugs, and calls a number from memory. "I met this guy in Tangier. He's a four-star general now. He knows the score."

This general might know the score, but he's not quick to answer the telephone. You wait for what seems like eternity, although that might just be because of Deadpool's horrible whistling. He's *so* shrill. It's maddening. Eventually someone answers, and you hear Deadpool's side of the conversation.

"Wade Wilson for General Penn. Tell him, 'Quetzalcoatl.' Yes, I'll hold. La la la la. I hate hold music. Especially army hold– Mark! It's Wade. This is a big one, like Lana Turner big. Alien weapon caches, seditious conspiracy, a wave of murders, even a subverted Ivy League colleague. Absolutely, a slaughter. On my favorite comfy sweater. Great! I'll email over the list. Thank you, Mark. Not just from me, from all of America. Next Thursday? Sounds delightful. I'll bring my six-iron, a gym-bag of tequila, and the 10th Airborne. Bye!"

You relax a little, knowing that the army are moving on some of the gun caches in their inimitable, high-impact way.

Take **+2 {WEAPONS DOWN}** and **+3 {CHAOS}**.

Now return to **216**.

254

The locker buzzes rudely at you, and the lights turn red. "Oh, that's just great, Sixlet. Smooth." Deadpool's fist flashes past your face, and the locker door crumples.

Before you can look inside, a band of thugs bursts in, fumbling for pistols. They don't even have a chance to fire, but by the time Deadpool's mopped them all up, he's got a nasty-looking new gash through the mask on his forehead and everything in the little room is smashed, including the locker.

Take +1 {CHAOS} and +1 {DISCORD}.

There's also a strong smell of gas, and it's getting stronger.

Deadpool fumbles around in the wreckage for a moment, and comes up with a torn piece of paper. He brandishes the note. "This says that the password for the One Family, Inc, facility on Bethesda Terrace Arcade is… illegible."

"Illegible?"

He balls the note up and throws it away. "It would have told us, but you set that buzzer off, and then those thugs jumped us. Now this warehouse is going to blow up as soon as that gas leak meets that smoldering waste bin over there. I don't mind, but if you don't want to explode, we should go."

"Where?"

"One Family must be more important than Second. But shouldn't it be First? Although First Family would sound like the president was crooked. Huh. Can you imagine? Thank the Lord that this is America." He winks really obviously.

If you want to research One Family, Inc, turn to **175**.
If you'd rather head straight over to Central Park, turn
to **48**.

255

This isn't just a storage warehouse, it's an entire distribution
operation. It might be deserted at this moment, but clearly
a bunch of people work here shipping things out. There's a
bewildering variety of crates addressed to locations across
the northeast. This cannot be good.

"This is *amazing!* Sixie, are you thinking what I'm
thinking?"

You squash your first reply, in favor of caution. "That…
depends."

"We can send guns to anyone!"

Of course. "I'm not sure–"

"Come on! The X-Men would be interested, Weasel can
rig a crate or two to explode, and I have a very important
friend who really needs a hand." He looks at you plaintively.
What do you say?

"The X-Men should be OK." Turn to **227**

"Exploding on use would be effective." Turn to **123**.

"It is nice to help friends." Turn to **54**.

"We really need to get going. Sorry." Turn to **232**.

256

You risk a few moments to examine some of the broken crates in the left-hand side of the warehouse. There's all sorts of general paramilitary nonsense – turtlenecks, webbing belts, canteens, battery packs, all of it predictably black – but there are also a lot of things that look very much like phasers from a certain popular space fiction franchise.

"Chitauri guns," Deadpool says. He sounds satisfied. "Want one?"

"What?" You can take an **[Alien Weapon]** if you want.

"We should sabotage some of these," he says. "It might help someone get lucky down the line."

It's easy enough, and the two of you spend five minutes sabotaging a few dozen weapons.

Take **+1 {NOBBLED GUNS}**.

> If you now have three Alien items in your inventory, turn immediately to **266**.
>
> To investigate the right aisles, turn to **146**.
>
> To scope out the shipping area you can see at the back, turn to **255**.
>
> Head straight for the command suites? Turn to **232**.

257

You look around for a fire extinguisher, and spot one standing behind the buffet table. Perfect. Time for Plan B. You grab it, heft it over your shoulder, and charge at one of the sculptures shouting: "Free the bees! Free the bees!"

Once there, you turn to face the room. "This is a blow for Apian Liberation!" you shout at the aghast faces. "Bees are life! Free the bees!"

You hammer the extinguisher into the middle of the sculpture, a worrying bas-relief of some desolate ocean island seething with, well, things. There's a loud *clunk*. It doesn't seem to do any damage, but you strike again, this time doing your best to use the sculpture to smash the top off the extinguisher. Woah, go Six!

An instant later, you're engulfed in powder. The room fills with shouts of alarm and confusion. Deadpool's hand appears, holding a pass-card and beckoning, and you let him lead you out.

Take **+1 MERC** and **+1 {CHAOS}**, and the ACHIEVEMENT: *They Love Me In That Buffet*.

You have a clear moment. Deadpool swipes the card, and the door makes a clicking sound. There's a big red button next to the door as well though.

If you tug on the door, turn to **160**.

If you push the button, turn to **55**.

258

Deadpool stares at you. "Call *who?*"

"He's the greatest hero New York has. He can foul up Hammerhead's plans." You are met with unfriendly silence. "Look, you wanted me to make unpredictable decisions for you. This is as unpredictable as it gets."

He sighs. "Fine. For you, Six. Appreciate it."

Take +1 {DISCORD}.

Deadpool punches a number, which picks up quickly. His side of the conversation is curt – he's clearly trying to convey the sense of the problem in as few words as possible. "Yes. Hi... Hammerhead... Chitauri guns, caches of them... Assassinations... I have locations. Yes, and proof." He groans. "Yes, P, I am asking for your help. Please help me. Yes, that did hurt. No, I'm not apologizing for that. Don't be greedy."

Make a persuasion test. Roll one die, and add your **MOUTH** and, if you have any, your {ORG SEC}. If you have {CENTRAL CRATER} of 1, subtract 1 from your total – Spider-Man was very fond of Central Park.

Score 8 or more: Spider-Man agrees to help wholeheartedly. Take +2 {WEAPONS DOWN}, +1 {CASH DOWN}, and -1 FOCUS because Deadpool is seething.

7 or less: It takes a long time bring him round even a little, but Spider-Man says he'll take time out from some critically important mission to have a look at it. Take +1 {WEAPONS DOWN}, +1 {OUT OF TIME}, and -2 FOCUS for Deadpool's utter frustration.

Now turn to **216**.

259

Deadpool carefully pulls a chunk of dead person from the stack, but you can immediately see it's the wrong bit. A moment later, the limb segments collapse in a gross heap, some splattering off the table and onto the floor.

Jengarm shakes his head. "Shame. You are little bit too clumsy, I think. Much promise, however. Do not feel bad. I am master."

"Good game," Deadpool nods.

"Eh, not bad. Now, we fight." Jengarm pulls a shotgun from beneath the table – it must have been clipped there – and draws a long, savage-looking scimitar from somewhere beneath his smoking jacket. Then he picks up the table and sends it flying, moving in to attack. He moves like a raging landslide. One way or another, this will be over swiftly.

This is a quick, brutal fight.

Start your {PENALTY} at 0.

If you have {CASINO OUTRAGE} of 2 or more, take +1 {PENALTY}.

If you have {ROLLING STONE} of 4 or more, take +1 {PENALTY}.

If you have {CHAOS} of 6 or more, take +1 {PENALTY}.

Now roll two dice, add your MERC, and subtract your {PENALTY}.

If the total is at least 11, you win.

Did you win?

> Yes: turn to **283**.
>
> No: turn to **152**.

With Deadpool there to give you a boost up, you manage to scrabble over the metal gate and lower yourself down the other side without incident. The gates sway and groan worryingly, but they don't fall. Deadpool swarms over without the least hesitation.

Take **+1 MERC**.

You find yourself in a sprawling, overgrown delivery yard. There are various rusted-out trucks and other pieces of machinery. Some look oddly to have stained ceramic segments, and one gives the impression of floating, but it must be just the long grass. When an ancient crane seems, for a moment, to turn to watch you, you're certain that your nerves are getting the better of you. There are a couple of intact structures nearby.

To try the warehouse, turn to **77**.

To try the once-red shed, turn to **228**.

"Hey, how about we talk to the bartender?" you suggest. Deadpool shrugs. The two of you make your way to the bar. All the other customers are still staring at you.

"Hello, gentlemen," the bartender says. She has a bright smile, a badge that says *Vera*, and a noticeable European accent. Polish, maybe? "What will it be?"

Deadpool produces ten bucks from somewhere you prefer not to think about, and slides it over. "Tequila."

"Sure." Vera sets up a couple of shot glasses, and pulls a bottle off the shelf in front of her.

"We're looking for information on Second Family," you say.

"No one has to get hurt," Deadpool adds.

She pours the tequila, still smiling, and for a moment, you're not sure if she heard you.

Make a persuasion test. Roll one die, and add your **MOUTH** to it.

If you and Deadpool drink your shots while she's considering the situation, they give you **+1** to **MERC** and **-1** to **FOCUS** for the next roll only.

6 or more: Vera shrugs, says, "Benny, clear your boys out," and ducks behind the bar. A number of the thugs get up and leave. No one says a thing. Turn to **220**.

5 or less: Vera grins nastily, shouts, "We got a live one, guys!", then ducks behind the bar. Turn to **229**.

262

The Timberline Suite isn't exactly high art, but it is a lot classier than the rest of this place. Inside, you find yourself mingling with a surprisingly upscale crowd – ugly middle-aged men and gorgeous young women dripping with wealth, obvious bodyguards bred for imposing size, a smattering of predatory men and women of various ages too stinking rich to bother displaying it, and a sprinkle of young, narcissistic influencers for seasoning. The great and the good of southern New Jersey, basically.

"This room is packed with murderous thugs and hey, that's Barry the Slime." Deadpool is pointing directly at a chunky, aging guy with a face full of anger issues.

The room falls silent, the bodyguards ready to pounce. A good chunk of the crowd are looking to Barry for a reaction. Only the influencers seem confused, but then they almost always do.

"I know you," the man growls, his voice pure Jersey Italian. "You're that merc. Little merc, there's a hundred witnesses to this slander. My lawyers–"

"You're a twisted, pathetic joke, Slimy. A broken, soulless husk waiting for death. Just another dumb, scum-sucking bottom-feeder without honor or charm or even humanity. You're nobody and nothing, just like your mama was."

Wow, now Barry does *not* look happy.

Make an intimidation test. Roll one die, and add your **MOUTH** to it.

Total 7 or more: take **+1 MOUTH**.

4-6:   take **+1 {CASINO OUTRAGE}**.

1-3:   take **+2 {CASINO OUTRAGE}**.

While everyone is stunned, and Barry gasps for air, you can slip out.

To head back to the bar, turn to **270**.

To go play the slots, turn to **164**.

To head across the room and on into the auction showcase, turn to **206**.

263

The chaos dies down, and you do not appear to be injured. You look up from behind the jukebox. The bar is completely trashed. It's littered with bodies, some groaning, some worryingly motionless, and there is blood everywhere.

Take **+1 MERC**.

On top of the jukebox, magically intact, you spot a can of **[Carefully Unbranded High-Caffeine Drink]** – if your **FOCUS** is less than 3 at any point, consume this for **+2 FOCUS**. Next to it is a **[Tasty Energy Bar]** – if your **MERC** is less than 3, consume for **+2 MERC**). You may take either or both with you, but remember you can only carry five items at a time.

Deadpool is on the floor, his legs wrapped around the neck of a particularly big, unhappy-looking thug. Behind them, your eyes drift over a poster that reads "Straczinsky A1B2C3 – America's Best Big Classy Cider Cup." The gore splattering it detracts from the effect.

"I can snap your neck," Deadpool is saying, "or you can tell me about Second Family. Or both." He flexes a little more.

The thug shrieks. "No! No!"

"No to which?"

"Don't kill me! You want One Family, Inc. Second is one of our, uh their divisions. There's a place in Bethesda Terrace Arcade in Central Park. You said you wouldn't kill me."

Deadpool lets the guy go and leads you outside, while the guy tries to catch his breath. You can hear sirens approaching from several directions. "Let's get going," he says.

To research One Family, Inc, turn to **175**.

To head straight over to Central Park, turn to **48**.

264

The controller hurries over towards the two of you, looking nervous but resolute. She's a stern-faced woman in her fifties, clearly no one to be trifled with. At least, not in the normal world where things make sense. Before she gets a chance to speak, though, Deadpool grabs her, whirls her around, and shoves her into a huge electronic screen. There's a loud crash, and a shower of sparks. The room erupts into screaming chaos. Alarms start blaring, the lights dim, and the operators leap up to run wildly for the exits. One of them, a greasy little guy, shoots you a peculiarly venomous look for someone supposedly terrified.

"Someone is using the subway to smuggle guns,"

Deadpool tells the dazed woman. "You're going to help us find them. I suggest you say 'Yes.'"

The woman nods. "Yes?"

He lets her down, and she limps over to a huge screen filled with a baffling maze of data. "What am I looking for?" she asks.

Test your **FOCUS** – roll one die, and add your **FOCUS** to it. What is the total?

5 or more: turn to **196**.

4 or less: turn to **277**.

265

The panel lights up as you find the series of connections to power the system. The back of the closet slides quietly away to reveal a stretch of ladder.

"Nice work, Sixpert," Deadpool says, eyeing the flimsy false wall. "You did great."

Climbing up, you come into a large space that's divided into a series of sections by a network of bars and openings. Bars are retracting and opening continuously, leading to an ever-changing maze. You're going to have to try to find your way through this bewildering labyrinth.

This is a maze minigame!

Start at the node marked "IN". In each node, roll one die and leave by the circle next to that number.

If you don't like your roll, you may re-roll the die, but only twice in total. If your **FOCUS** is 6 or more, you may add a third re-roll.

If you have a [Shining Icosahedron], you may alter any one roll by up to 3, but doing so destroys the item.

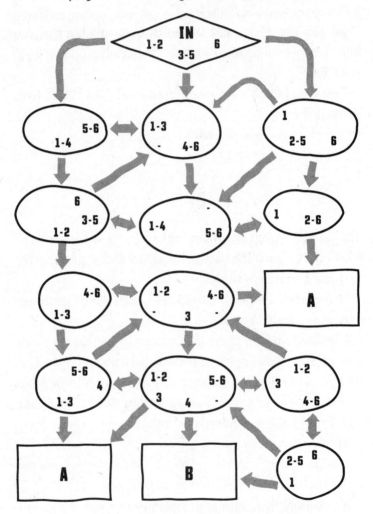

If you come to a node marked "A", turn to **65**.
If you come to the node marked "B", turn to **159**.

266

You hear a nasty whining noise as your commandeered alien items react to each other. A moment later, there's a flash of light. Deadpool takes the worst of it, and is flung half an aisle away, but you're still dazed on the floor when he limps up to you, frowning.

Remove all the Alien items from your inventory. Take **-1 MERC** and **+1 {DISCORD}**, and the ACHIEVEMENT: *Greed is Good*.

Now, to try the shipping area at the back of the room, turn to **255**.

To head for the command suites, turn to **232**.

267

Bypassing the puzzle will cost you a little of your accumulated puzzle score, and it's worse if you don't have the **[Magnifying Glass]**. Are you sure?

To give the puzzle a go, turn back to **163**.

To really bypass the puzzle, take **-1 {PUZZLER}**, and if you don't have the **[Magnifying Glass]**, also take **-2 MOUTH**. Now turn to **265**.

268

"Be charming," you mutter to Deadpool.

He tilts his head at you. "Moi?"

The receptionist is here now. "May I ask what it going on?"

"I need to speak to the assistant director in charge. My name is Deadpool. You might have heard of me. I have evidence of a national plot to unleash a wave of terrorist attacks across the country – tomorrow."

Make a persuasion test. Roll one die and add your **MOUTH**.

7 or more: The AD actually comes out, and Deadpool is mostly pleasant and coherent. He shows the various files he has on his phone, and emails a copy. The FBI will be on the case! Take **+1 {WEAPONS DOWN}**. Have you seen their budgets lately?

6 or less: The receptionist takes some details and promises faithfully to get them in front of the AD as soon as humanly possible. She is not being entirely honest.

Return to the safe-house by turning to **216**.

269

There are eleven possibilities where at least one die is a 1. Only one of those possibilities has the other die as a 1. So it's 1 in 11. Sorry, but you do partially disable the lock.

"Great work, Mariachi," Deadpool says.

The left-hand cupboard opens, showing you a rough map of the complex. You make a note of the route to the command center. There are also three identical lockers in this cupboard, and you have time to open and potentially loot just one of them.

To open locker one, turn to **226**.

To open locker two, turn to **248**.

To open locker three, turn to **84**.

270

The dim lighting and plastic cheer of the bar doesn't hide the desperate misery of the clientele. There is a long buffet table though, laden down with a wide selection of deep-fried surprises – wings, ribs, vegetable bits, fish, they've even got deep-fried cheese blocks and bite-size burritos. Every so often, there is also a tray of champagne flutes.

Deadpool's eyes have gone wide. "*Chimichangitas*," he breathes. "Has science gone too far?" He heads over to the burrito bites and grabs a handful. You couldn't stop him if you wanted to. Eventually, he stops, grabs a tray of champagne glasses, and brings it over. "I'm *really* thirsty now," he says.

But is this the right time for booze? If you indulge, take **+1 MERC, +1 MOUTH, -2 FOCUS**, and set **{TIPSY}** to 1. If not, take **+1 {DISCORD}** to reflect Deadpool's regrets. Either way, time to move on.

To try the slots, turn to **164**.

To investigate the auction, turn to **262**.

271

The ride up to Hammerhead's lair is short and smooth. It's not a tall building, after all. The elevator is thankfully free of muzak, so how evil can this guy really be? (Quite impressively evil, if you were wondering.)

Be honest, now. Do you have six or more items with you?

Yes? Take the ACHIEVEMENT: *Compulsive Hoarder*.

No? Take the ACHIEVEMENT: *Frugal*.

Now let's be even more honest, hmm? Did you just tick off *both* of those achievements? If so, add the ACHIEVEMENT: *Terminally Indecisive*. You probably don't need to worry about the word "terminally". We haven't asked you to make an achievement test yet, have we? Exactly. Nothing to worry about.

Nothing at all. Are you {SPORE-SEEDED}, by the way? No, no, just making conversation. Perhaps you should move swiftly on.

The elevator door opens onto a large, luxurious room decorated like a 1920s Las Vegas executive suite. There's the immense oak desk, the leather desk chair, the glass and chrome card table, and lots and lots of marble with gold trim. Tacky.

Oh, and an entire squad of terrifying gangsters in red three-piece suits all carrying high-tech Tommy guns. Hammerhead is in the middle of the squad. Blue three-piece suit with black pinstripes and matching tie, white spats over black wingtip brogues, and a face carved from rage and greed. His forehead is way too wide, flaring out to flatten the top of his head. He's not particularly tall, but he seems to loom over the entire room.

"Joseph, my man!" Deadpool says brightly. "Hey, can I call you Joe? Sure I can. Well, Joey baby, it's been a time huh? Doing well for yourself, I see. It's a long way from Little Odessa or whatever."

"Wilson, ya lousy, good-for-nothing scumbag! Youse cost me a packet, and I'm gonna enjoys cutting ya to shreds again and again."

"It's important to have an interest," Deadpool says earnestly. "Helps make you a well-rounded person." He pauses. "Well-rounded. Ha. As in unlike your head, pigeye."

Hammerhead grinds his teeth together. "I'm gonna love this. And when I gets bored of ya screams, I'll have my boys take over. Youse gonna have a long, agonizing life."

"You had me at 'long', Josephine."

"Grease this mouthy goon, boys."

Deadpool steps forward, and he's more menacing than you've ever seen him. The thugs flinch back a little. "I've slaughtered *hundreds* of you idiots in this book alone." His voice is little more than a cruel growl. "I know mallet-face is shouty, but I will garb myself in your twitching entrails and dance the Pachanga. You cannot kill me." Several thugs open fire, and bullets hit him across his torso. You can make out the slow, evil grin under his mask. "Thank you for that demonstration. You poor fools have precisely one path to survival. Step. Aside. Now."

Make an intimidation test. Roll a die and add your **MOUTH**. If you have a [Clown Mask] for Deadpool to pull on for his speech, add **+2** to your total.

Score 10 or more: As Hammerhead gibbers in fury, the thugs step aside. Turn to **201** immediately.

9 or less: The red-suited gangsters ignore Deadpool's warning, and a battle erupts. This is the mook round of the final boss fight.

Round one: roll two dice and add your **MERC**. If the total is at least 12, you win the first round.

Round two: roll two dice and add your **MERC**. If the total is at least 12, you win the second round.

Round three: roll two dice and add your **MERC**. If the total is at least 12, you win the third round.

If you won at least two rounds, turn to **244**.

If you lost at least two rounds, turn to **30**.

272

With a satisfying click, the locker pops open. "And they told me math would never be useful in the real world," Deadpool says.

"Who?"

"My teachers. I don't think they liked me much."

"It's difficult to imagine," you say.

"I was a cherub. Well, I had a longbow and burning arrows. Same thing, right?"

There are two things inside. One is a note saying that last Thursday's password for the One Family, Inc facility on Bethesda Terrace Arcade is "Swordfish." Typical. The other item is a set of complex instructions for a cunning foosball table lock, which you memorize.

Take **+1 {PUZZLER}** and set **{FOOSBALL LOCK}** to 1.

"One Family." You show Deadpool the note.

"One is better than Second. But shouldn't it be First? Although First Family would sound like the president was crooked. Huh. Can you imagine? Thank the Lord that this is America." He winks really, really obviously.

If you want to research One Family, Inc, turn to **175**.

If you'd rather head straight over to Central Park, turn to **48**.

273

The left-hand corridor ends in a doorway to your right and a sliding shutter straight ahead. Deadpool looks at it for a moment, then easily lifts the shutter to reveal a thick metal security grille and, on the other side, a small room containing a bunch of gun safes. He rattles the grille optimistically, but it's very firmly in place. It does look like it could recede into the floor, but there's no sign of any activation mechanism.

"I might be able to batter this down," Deadpool says.

"Or we could go through this handy door," you counter.

"But–"

"You've got pistols, swords, and at least one grenade, and that's just the things I can see strapped to you," you say. "Is it really worth beating your way through metal bars and forcing open a safe just for another gun?"

Deadpool pouts at you.

"Is it?" you repeat.

"No." He sounds sad, like a child forced to eat his broccoli.

"There will be more guns," you promise.

To take the door on your right, turn to **292**.

To retrace your steps and try the left-hand corridor, turn to **221**.

Deadpool limps over and pulls you to your feet. The office is an orange-spackled disaster. The only thing still intact is a metal locker behind Palmetto's desk.

"What a senseless waste," Deadpool says as he picks his way across the room. "I liked that carpet. I bet it would have been amazing to roll around in. Did you know that if you snap all of your ribs, you can get really low to the ground? It's really interesting. Like learning to be a worm all over again."

You follow him to the shiny locker, trying not to look at the floor, the walls, or anything, really. Deadpool is holding an equally shiny key. Presumably he got it from Palmetto, because it opens the locker.

Inside is a monitor showing a network that stretches across the northeast. This base is part of the network, but it isn't even a major hub. Taped to the inside of the locker is a [Rusted Key], which you may take as one of your five items.

Deadpool groans. "'Cake,' he said. 'Nice and simple,' he said. Thor's twitchy black nasal hairs. This isn't a smuggling operation, it's a secret army."

"So we're not done?" you say.

"Done? We're not even started, Big Six." He pauses. "I mean, obviously we've started. This is the end of the first act. But we've got a lot to do." He studies the map for a minute or two. "There are three important sites marked on here: in Atlantic City, the Berkshires, and southern

Vermont. They're big and sparkly, anyway. Oh, and there's this." He points at a very big red button labeled *Autodestruct Sequence*. "Sweet, huh? It seems rude not to." He reaches for it.

If you let Deadpool press the Autodestruct button, well… red lights start flashing, and a siren begins blaring out a menacingly calm countdown. Hurrying out, you discover the siren is audible across Central Park, and everyone in five blocks is fleeing in terror. You and Deadpool are sprinting across Fifth Avenue when there's a titanic whump and the ground heaves you five feet into the air. Central Park is reduced to a very big crater. New York's property barons will frenzy in their haste to turn the beloved national icon into luxury apartments. Good work. Take **+3 {CHAOS}, +1 {CENTRAL CRATER}, +1 {IMPRESSIVELY RECKLESS}**, and the ACHIEVEMENT: *Landscaping*.

If not, Deadpool looks disappointed, you monster, but you leave quietly and Central Park gets to live on. For now. Probably for the best. Mark the ACHIEVEMENT: *Phase One Went Smoo-oothly*.

Now, the sparkly network sites are a casino in Atlantic City called The Golden Table, a supposedly-abandoned copper mine in the hills north of Brattleboro in Vermont, and Emma Frost's former Massachusetts Academy in Snow Valley, now a corporate retreat.

To head to Atlantic City, go to **237**.

To head to Brattleboro, go to **57**.

To head to Snow Valley, go to **73**.

275

The reporter must have Deadpool's number, because within thirty seconds, he's on the air. You listen with growing horror.

"This is so exciting! Deadpool, you're live on NYNN 104. Welcome to the show!"

"Please, Trish, call me Wade."

"Wade. Tell us, what are you up to today?"

"Oh, it's baaaad." He turns to give you a big, conspiratorial wink. "New York is full of incredibly dangerous alien weapons, and the bad guys are going to turn them on the public any minute now in a horrific wave of total slaughter. It's going to be carnage, Trish." He turns again, and flashes you an excited thumbs up.

There's a moment of stunned silence. *"Wow. Uh. Are you sure, Wade?"*

"Absolutely certain. Daredevil told me all about it, and Six and I are going to try to stop it. Have you ever seen entire office buildings get sliced into confetti by unstoppable energy beams, Trish? I haven't."

What have you done? You take your headset off for a moment, and pinch the bridge of your nose. The pilot looks horrified, darting glances left and right like he wants to make a run for it, but he keeps the 'copter in place.

Deadpool is still gesticulating, and you warily put your headset back on. "No, it's absolutely true, Trish. Spider-Man is *terrified* of water. Thinks he's going to get flushed down the drain. He absolutely stinks, all the time. We stopped inviting him to parties because the smell was just unbearable, like something had died and then been left out in the sun for weeks."

Urgently you get Deadpool's attention and make wild cutting motions across your own throat, then tap your wrist repeatedly. He does get the message and finish talking, but it's too late. The black helicopter has vanished.

Take **+2 {CHAOS}**, **+1 MOUTH** and the ACHIEVEMENT: *Slanderous*.

If you have **{SUSPICIOUS NAME}** of 1+ and want to use that lead, turn to **86**.

Or, if you haven't already:

To try underground routes, turn to **179**.

To try surface routes, turn to **43**.

276

You head along the left-hand tunnel, and after a couple of twists, find yourself approaching a rough-hewn circular chamber.

"Easiest maze ever," Deadpool says. "You're the good-luck albatross around my throat, Six."

"I don't–"

"Good work."

If you have **[Milk]** and **[Cookies]**, eat them now, and take **+1 MOUTH** for your stubborn lack of faith in our stage directions. Also take the ACHIEVEMENT: *Obtuse*.

Next, you enter the chamber. There's a shimmer, and you discover that the walls are draped with regularly-spaced crimson drapes. Flickering candles on copper candelabras stand between them. A complex design of circles, triangles, and occult sigils cast in bright copper is set into the floor, and it seems to be humming nastily.

No, wait. It's not the design. The humming is emanating from a big, shining, polychromatic octopus you only just noticed. The humming deepens and intensifies, and a tentacle lashes out.

This is a strange fight against the Psychic Octopus.

Round one: roll two dice and add two for the octopus, with a maximum of 12. Then roll two dice and add your **FOCUS**. If your total is more than the Octopus's total, you win.

Round two: roll two dice and add four for the octopus, with a maximum of 13. Then roll two dice and add your **FOCUS** or your **MOUTH**, whichever is bigger. If your total is more than the Octopus's total, you win.

Round three: roll two dice and add six for the octopus, with a maximum of 11. Then roll two dice and add your **FOCUS** or your **MERC**, whichever is smaller. If your total is more than the Octopus's total, you win.

If you lost two or more rounds, take **-2** to one of either **MERC**, **MOUTH**, or **FOCUS**, your choice.

As the octopus dissolves into an indescribable fetor and a small puddle of slime, you see a shimmering portal to another world come into being in the center of the circle. There's also a **[Sparkling Icosahedron]** lying in the slime that you may take.

Now, to press on into the tunnels, turn to **224**.

To head to another world, turn to **14**.

277

A loud siren starts wailing, coming from a complicated-looking metal box covered with green LEDs over in one corner, down by the floor and partially hidden by boxes. The controller looks over at it. "What the heck is that thing? Is this something to do with you clowns?"

"Hey, clowns are an important–" Deadpool begins.

Everything switches off, and you are plunged into darkness. Someone shrieks in your ear. "Someone." Sure.

The lights flicker back on, dimmer. All the displays are blue-screened, all the terminals static. The controller swears, runs to a console, and starts pounding keys. Nothing happens. She grabs a cellphone, her face falling.

"It wasn't us," you say quickly. "Honestly."

"Doesn't matter," she says. "It's all fried. The whole network. This is a disaster." She swears again. "Hackers are claiming they did this? What kind of hacker group is 'Second Family'? Ever hear of them?"

"No," Deadpool says. "But we'll find them."

Take +1 {SUSPICIOUS NAME}, +2 {CHAOS}, and +1 {NO (SUB)WAY}.

There's a [Train Lever] here that you can pick up in the commotion, if you have room.

To follow up on your lead, turn to **86**.

Or, if you haven't already:

To try surface routes, turn to **43**.

To try air routes, turn to **91**.

278

Despite the constant bantering back and forth with Deadpool, Weasel somehow manages to find some information. "I've found a schematic from the city records. It's absolute rubbish, just pure fantasy, but it does show a side entrance through a subway tunnel. Looks to me like the complex goes under the lake, so be careful? Drowning sucks."

"It's quite peaceful, actually," Deadpool says. "Once you stop fighting."

"Water-boarding was horrible."

"Sure, but I was *torturing* you. It's supposed to be horrible. If it was fun, they'd call it kinky."

You look at your drink, which smells indescribably nasty. "We should really get going," you say.

> If {NO (SUB)WAY} is 1 or more and you want to try the side door, turn to **182**.
>
> Otherwise, turn to **48**.

279

Welcome from *She-Hulk Goes to Murderworld*! We just hope you know what you're in for.

Set your **MERC, MOUTH, FOCUS** and {CHAOS} to 5 each. Cross off all of your equipment.

Do you have {I WAS ONCE A MAN} of 1?

Yes: That was very odd. Take the ACHIEVEMENT: *Twisty* and turn to **224**.

No: Turn to **35**, but you can ignore the stat instructions there.

280

You head over to the buffet, scoop up several jumbo shrimp, and quickly fling them at the heads of various art admirers. There's a man not too far from you, and you shriek, "Stop it you *freak!*", grab a tub of salsa, and empty it over his head. While he falls back into the table, you take the opportunity to push an elegant-looking lady face-first into the chocolate fountain, throw a punch-filled crystal bowl straight up into the air, and run around screaming like you were on fire.

By the time everyone gets over their shock, there's too much havoc to make sense of. The guards step away from the door, and Deadpool breezes past them. You drop under a buffet table and pop out the other end quietly, joining him.

Killer moves, Six! Take **+1 MOUTH** and **+1 {CHAOS}**, and the ACHIEVEMENT: *They Love Me In That Buffet*.

You have a clear moment. Deadpool swipes the card, and the door makes a clicking sound. There's a big red button next to the door as well though.

If you tug on the door, turn to **160**.

If you push the button, turn to **55**.

281

You quickly follow the sign towards Administration and soon pass through a door into a normal looking office – normal, that is, if this was the late Eighties, and your office was in a fallout shelter.

"Oh, hello. Who are you?" The speaker is a woman in her thirties. She looks nice, but her sweater is grotesque. Is that a *mermaid*? You refuse to think about the squid.

"I'm Deadpool," says Deadpool cheerfully. "You may have heard of me."

She thinks it over. "No." She looks him up and down. "Are you Robbie's replacement?"

"Yes," you say quickly. "Hail, uh–" You have no idea who to hail.

She peers at you. "Hail. Right. I'll need my umbrella, then. I have to, um..." She gets up and bumbles off.

Make a fast-talk test. Roll one die, add your **MOUTH**, and subtract your {CENTRAL ALERT} score, if any.

Total is 4 or more: She's gone for coffee. You have a moment.

3 or less: She's gone for help. Take **+1** {CENTRAL ALERT}.

There are a couple of cupboards on one of the walls, under a large propaganda-style poster of happy children playing in a sweet family park. Between the cupboards is a keypad.

This is a puzzle, in the form of a question. Imagine that you roll two normal six-sided dice without looking at the result. At least one of them comes up "1". What is the probability that the other is also a "1"?

1 in 6? Turn to **194**.

1 in 11? Turn to **67**.

1 in 23? Turn to **269**.

1 in 36? Turn to **81**.

282

There's hubbub in the background, but right at the moment, your way is clear. Fortunately it's just a short trip through the steam tunnels to the storage area.

Well. You're now in a cavernous space, far larger than you expected. It's absolutely filled with storage racks, all of them holding anonymous wooden crates. There's a sketchy site diagram on the wall that shows the approximate way to the command suites.

"Two hundred crates in just that corner, or more, or less, or something," Deadpool says, sounding awed.

"Nothing we can do in time would be able to sabotage all of this," you say.

"Two important points."

"Oh?"

"We don't know how many of the guns are here yet – and we're about to be killed."

He's right on both counts. A pack of security guards with machine-guns are spread out around you, amongst the aisles, and they're about to open fire. As you drop behind a pile of boxes, Deadpool leaps up into the air, spinning like a top, his pistols already blazing. You really need to get some ear defenders. This is getting ridiculous.

This is a simple fight.

Round one: roll two dice and add your **MERC**. If the total is at least 9, you win the first round.

Round two: roll two dice and add your **MERC**. If the total is at least 9, you win the second round.

That was a lot of machine-gun fire. Take **-1 MERC** for each round you lost.

When you poke your head back up, dizzy from the noise, Deadpool is posing on top of a pile of dead, dying, unconscious, injured, and/or utterly terrified guards. He could be trying to poorly mimic Rodin's "The Thinker." The area around the fight is comprehensively trashed – toppled shelving, splintered boxes, heaps of packing material, and all sorts of supplies. You don't know how long you have, but for now, the coast is clear.

Would you like to:

Investigate the left aisles? Turn to **256**.

Investigate the right aisles? Turn to **146**.

Head straight for the command suites? Turn to **232**.

283

The fight barely lasts ten seconds, but after several loud clashes of metal and a shotgun blast that leaves your head ringing, Jengarm is on his face on the floor with one of Deadpool's swords at his neck.

"Be easy," the Russian says, presumably to his men. "You fight like greased *prokaznyk*, Deadpool. Most deadly. I sell information for life, yes?"

"Of course," Deadpool says reassuringly. "You're a craftsman, Jengarm, an artist. How could I kill you?"

"Good. Is deal. Controller for region is–"

"Wait, 'controller'? You're not the boss?"

"Me?" He laughs, sincerely amused. "No. I keep art and turn fools into money. Boss of whole country I do not know. But controller of my northeast network part, I know. Professor of Folklore at college named Coreham, near Boston. Ivy League, very fancy. His name is Hope. Mudak. He knows where to find boss, or so he boasts."

You wait for the authorities to come and take the Russian and his men off your hands, then you set off for Boston. Note the ACHIEVEMENT: *I'm a Machine*.

To scout out Coreham College, turn to **287**.

To just go straight there, turn to **148**.

284

"What about that alien gun?" you ask.

"Ooo, yes, let's give it a try." Deadpool pulls out the device, and fiddles with it. "It has an 'Esgotar' setting, apparently. That's got to be good, right?"

Deadpool aims the device at the lobby and presses a button. There's a horrific explosion of light and sound, and you're flung ten feet down the sidewalk. When you finally look up, you see Deadpool cradling a blackened hand. Past him, the former lobby is a ruin of scorched rubble and broken bodies.

The [Alien Weapon] is gone. Remove it from your inventory.

Make a luck test. Roll one die as you pick your way through the mess. On a 4 or more, you spot a [Security Pass] on a recumbent guard. You may take it.

Now, if you want to use the elevators onwards, turn to **249**.

If you would rather take the stairs, turn to **171**.

285

This break room holds a bunch of new couches, some low tables, two coffee machines, and a foosball table. It's ... OK.

There are a half-dozen bright yellow lab-coats, hanging on a long coat rack. If you need [Disguises], you may take them.

Do you have {FOOSBALL LOCK} of 1? If so, curiously, you can use the table to duplicate the odd sequence of moves you saw, and a black and gold [Luckstone] pops out of the machine's tray. You may take it, and later crush it to automatically win any one non-combat test.

You could also choose to play Deadpool at foosball. Despite his boasts about being the King of the Foosball Monsters, he's not that great.

Make a luck test. Roll one die.

1-3: Deadpool wins and won't shut up about it. Take **+1 MERC** and **-1 FOCUS**.

4-6: You win, and Deadpool sulks. Take **+1 FOCUS** and **-1 MERC**.

Now, to go the nearby corridor, turn to **149**.

To go into the canteen, turn to **290**.

286

Hammerhead advances on Deadpool, fists raised. You hear a helicopter quickly getting closer outside, then a loudspeaker blares out: "This is the NYPD! Put down your weapons. Response squads are converging on your position. We will open fire with weapons capable of harming powered individuals if you do not surrender. You have thirty seconds to comply."

Hammerhead snarls. "I'm gonna find ya, Wilson, youse and the rat. I will *destroy* youse." He goes to a cupboard door, opens it to reveal a drop-shaft, and steps through. The door slams behind him, and you hear bars chunk into place.

There is a wave of gang violence in the days that follow, but it's concentrated in the Midwest and the South. You didn't save everyone, but you did prevent a major disaster.

Achievement: *Snatching Defeat From the Jaws of Victory*.

Final score: 2 stars.

The end.

You're close to Boston when Deadpool raises Weasel on the phone.

"Weas, it's been very strange. What can you tell me about Coreham College?"

"Hey Wade. Give me a moment. That dork of yours still alive?"

"Yes!" you snap.

"So far, Companion the Sixth," Weasel says. "So far. Right. Coreham. Built in 1888 by some poet who moved from England. Liberal arts, mostly. Well respected, very rich, unusually good occult and folklore library."

"Evil?" Deadpool asks.

"Utterly. Just riddled with secret societies, dozens of student deaths covered up every year – always the poorer students, of course – as are the scores of campus dogsbodies who go missing. They've got sightings of a vile monster in the swimming pool, rumors of sacrifices in the woods, funds invested in companies who specialize in burning down the Amazon, all your usual. The only reason they don't hire out mercenaries to dictators and Colombian death-squads is that they don't have any. Great cafeteria."

"What about a Professor Hope?"

"Been there twenty years, crusty old frogspawn of a man. Boring."

"Maybe not. I'll let you know."

"Have fun wrecking the place, you two."

"Later, Weasel."

Not long after, you arrive. Coreham College is a beautiful campus university in the Collegiate Gothic style, red brick with white-trimmed arched windows, steeply gabled roofs, crenelated towers, and cupolas. It's set in several acres of carefully kept grounds, lawns and groves punctuated with elegant paths and, here and there, fountains. It's busy with expensively attired students bustling to and fro, many of whom are clutching books or carrying heavy bags.

"Hey! *Hey!* Deadpool!"

You both look over at the excited shouting. A young man is rushing up, grinning widely.

"Deadpool! It is you!"

Deadpool bows. "In the flesh."

"Omigosh, I'm your biggest fan. I *have* to stab you in the face. Please, let me stab you in the face!"

Wait, what? You just know Deadpool will agree.

To let Deadpool get stabbed, turn to **5**.

To protest this senseless violence, turn to **94**.

288

"Hey Jughead! Looking buff, big guy. Don't worry, this is all for a good cause. So there's this network of murderers, and Hammerhead's smuggling alien weapons, but it's all about organized crime when you get down to it, and they've got – no, Six, I've got this, shh, shhhh – yeah, it's under the Ivy League, but they've been using black helicopters. There's a casino in Atlantic City, you know, and they've taken over that mutant school and turned it into a lair and day-spa, and–"

Make a babble test. Roll one die, and add your **MOUTH** to it.

If the total is 5 or less, Juggernaut growls, and swings the sort of punch that can send tanks into orbit. Turn immediately to **167**.

If the total is 6 or 7, Juggernaut lets Deadpool wind down, then shakes his head. "You're pathetic, Wilson. Stop wrecking my city." He gets on his bike and leaves, shaking his head in disgust all the way. Take **-1 MOUTH**.

If the total is 8 or more, over the course of five minutes, Deadpool somehow gives Juggernaut the idea that the X-Mansion has been taken over by Viking terrorists. The super hero swears, leaps back onto his bike, and speeds off to the attack. Take **+2 {CHAOS}**.

Assuming you're still here, it's time to prepare for the main event. You can call Weasel for some research first – though this will use up precious time – or you can go straight to the safe-house.

> To research Hammerhead's core personnel, turn to **238**.
>
> To research his network's operational structure, turn to **70**.
>
> To head to the safe-house, turn to **216**.

289

"Let's make an entrance," you suggest.

Deadpool's mask crinkles around the eyes, and you can sense the massive proud grin beneath it. He draws his swords, then charges for the door and leaps at it, foot out. The door blasts off its hinges and he vanishes into the bar in a cloud of splinters, yelling incoherently. You dash in after him.

You find him standing on the broken door in the middle of the bar, surrounded by a ring of muscular thugs with pistols aimed at him. There's got to be twenty of them. One, taller, burlier, and dumber than the rest, takes a step forward. "Bad move, pal." He sounds like a Scorsese stereotype.

Deadpool turns back to you. "Scare them off or start slicing?"

If you want to try intimidation, turn to **158**.

If you want to start fighting, turn to **229**.

290

The canteen has a service counter and swinging kitchen door at one end, a bank of vending machines at the other end, and a jumble of cheap tables and plastic chairs in between. There's no one at the counter, but the machines are well-stocked. Deadpool spots an instant burrito machine and buries his sword into it, cursing furiously. The machine emits a strangled blare.

A couple of guys in blue suits rush in. They see Deadpool, and begin blasting away with their pistols.

This is an easy fight.

Round one: roll two dice and add your **MERC**. If the total is at least 12, you win the first round.

Round two: roll two dice and add your **MERC**. If the total is at least 12, you win the second round.

If you lost any rounds, take **-1 MERC**.

Now, to try the kitchen, turn to **104**.

To follow signs to the break room, turn to **285**.

To go out into the corridor, turn to **149**.

291

"I'm not sure he'll be much use, but we can try," Deadpool says. He dials a number. You hear someone on the other end, but you can't tell what they're saying. Deadpool gives you side-eye before replying.

"This is Deadpool. Well, I prefer 'rugged anti-hero,' but sure, the *merc*. I need to talk to, uh, the big man himself. Yes, I'm sure he's extremely busy. No, it can't wait. This is a literally matter of life and death. Like, *megadeath*. Thousands of corpses all over the country. What? No, they're not coming back to life, they're not dead yet. Soon! Wow, that's nihilistic. Look, please, just tell him it's genuinely really urgent. Fine." He looks at you. "Mr. Lah-di-dah is in an important meeting and will I hold, honestly, like this is a sales call for luncheon meat."

The voice says something again.

"What?" He mutes the mic. "He says to tell me he's got every confidence in me to handle the situation, that I've got this, and that I'm a clever and resourceful professional who won't let him down. Jerk." He unmutes the call. "Tell him he's uglier than he hopes he is." He hangs up.

Take **+1 MOUTH** for the pep-talk. Now turn to **216**.

292

You go through the door into a large, open-plan space that feels a bit like an evil loft apartment, except for the whole being thirty feet underground thing. Professor Hope is at the back of the room, working with something on his desk, but between you and him are a heap of brutish campus security guards. Unlike the others you've seen, they're wearing black armbands, and they look like they work out compulsively as an alternative to trying to find a personality. They're carrying submachine-guns and billy clubs.

As you enter, the guards fan out into a semi-circle, and you hear their weapons readying. You drop behind the corner of the wall as Deadpool strolls into the eye of the kill-zone.

This is a moderate fight.

Round one: roll two dice and add your **MERC**. If the total is at least 11, you win the first round.

Round two: roll two dice, add your **MERC**, and add **+1** if you won round one.If the total is at least 12, you win the second round.

Round three: roll two dice, add your **MERC**, and add **+1** for each of the previous rounds you won. If the total is at least 13, you win the third round.

If you lost at least two rounds, turn to **214**.

If you won at least two rounds, turn to **156**.

293

That's some dedication to the cause of self-improvement. Well done. You both feel wonderful. Take an extra **+1** to **MERC**, **MOUTH**, and **FOCUS**, and **-1** to **{CHAOS}**. You're going to chew names and take gum, and no mistake.

Achievement: *My Best Me.*

If you *also* have at least 1 in each of **{CASH DOWN}**, **{NAMES DOWN}**, **{WEAPONS DOWN}**, and **{RESOURCE-FUL}**, take an extra **+1** to each of those qualities and the achievement: *One With Everything*, then turn to **3**.

Otherwise, press on to **243**.

294

You can tell you're outside the boss's office. The breakfast nook boasts six different types of tea, a pot of delicious-smelling coffee, three different types of bagel, eight types of donut, and a wide variety of jellies and savory spreads. You can grab a moment to relax and refuel here – you may choose to take **+1 MERC**, but also **+1 {CENTRAL ALERT}**.

To use the bathroom, turn to **90**.

To go meet the boss, turn to **191**.

295

This corridor is a bit less desolate than others you've seen so far. It's painted white, with reasonable carpet, and a line of light-colored wooden doors along its length. One is the door to the boiler room, but the others hold small nameplates.

To head to the boiler room, turn to **116**.

To try the door labeled *Dr Lundt*, turn to **233**.

To try the door labeled *Dr Smythe*, turn to **12**.

To try the door labeled *Store*, turn to **215**.

296

It seems like Deadpool is hammering on the steel security door for what feels like forever. Eventually it swings open fast, knocking him back into the room. Several guards with semi-automatics barge in, firing. Deadpool catches his balance, and leaps at them.

This is a simple fight.

Round one: roll one die and add your **MERC**. If the total is at least 6, you win the first round.

Round two: roll one die and add your **MERC**. If the total is at least 6, you win the second round.

If you lost both rounds, take **-1 MOUTH** from the shame of it all.

Leaving the security guards bleeding on the floor, you go through into a concrete corridor done out in fallout shelter chic. You're at a corner.

To go straight ahead, turn to **221**.

To head left, turn to **273**.

297

You come down into a claustrophobic network of ugly concrete steam tunnels. It's a far cry from the tasteful glass door in arcade. You clearly hear a gun being cocked, and realize that you've come down into the middle of a large group of well-armed security goons.

Take **+3 {CENTRAL ALERT}**.

This is a tricky fight.

Round one: roll two dice and add your **MERC**. If the total is at least 11, you win the first round.

Round two: roll two dice and add your **MERC**. If the total is at least 9, you win the second round.

If you win both rounds, Deadpool wipes out the guards before they can report clearly. Take **-1 {CENTRAL ALERT}**.

If you win one round, Deadpool gets a couple of fingers blown off by a lucky shot. Take **-1 MERC**.

If you lose both rounds, Deadpool gets turned into a bullet piñata before finally beating the last guy down with his broken wrist. Take **-1 MERC**, **-1 MOUTH**, and **-1 FOCUS**.

Bodies are everywhere, but you have a moment to breathe. Gore-coated signs on the tunnel walls point towards Administration one way and Storage the other. A spray of brain matter is dashed rather artistically over the admin sign.

If you want to try Administration, turn to **281**.

If you want to try Storage, turn to **282**.

298

You wait for a moment, sure the minions are about to raise alarms, or launch a spirited attack, or something. They don't. They continue to completely ignore you. It's a little embarrassing, and Deadpool is clearly offended, but you resolve to make the most of it and press on.

"Not even a sandwich," he complains.

Take **+1 {DISCORD}** and set **{MOOKIGNORE}** to 1.

If you want to get onto the conveyor belt, turn to **230**.

If you want to advance on solid ground, turn to **174**.

The library is ridiculously immense. It must cover an acre or more, and it looks to have at least three stories. The doors are all like vast, towering tombstones, and as you pass through them, your ears seem to deaden. You can still hear Deadpool whistling tunelessly beside you, but it's as if the noise is filtered through water. Which is an improvement.

You stride into a vast chamber crammed with row after row of heavy iron shelving. It's all packed full of books. A bit further in, there's a glade in the forest, and you can see a bit of a balcony of the floor above. It smells of dust, paper, and, oddly, bananas. You look around for assistance. There isn't any. No enquiries, no returns, no withdrawals – nothing but books.

"Hello?" Deadpool shouts.

You flinch, somehow expecting vicious repercussions. They don't come, but Deadpool fidgets quietly anyway.

Make an observation test. Roll one die, and add your **FOCUS** to it.

> Get a total of 7 or more: You spot a well-labeled map, and find Folklore. Turn to **209**.
>
> 6 or less: You've got nothing, so go try administration. Take +1 {GUARDS, GUARDS} and turn to **161**.

300

We hope you're not looking for the book's happy ending. This isn't the good old days any more and anyway, there are several possible endings. None of them are here. Sorry. (Not sorry.)

With the Academy boss crushed to a nasty pulp, the surviving minions are all too keen to be helpful. You get the impression that their service wasn't entirely voluntary.

"You need to go to Boston." The speaker, as graceful and well-dressed as the rest, has a thick Dutch accent and looks to be in his mid-twenties. "Professor Hope runs the Folklore department of Coreham College, just outside the city."

"He's running this army?" Deadpool asks hopefully.

The man shakes his head in wonder. "Truly, you are very ignorant."

Deadpool nods. "I blame Daredevil."

"The professor is the administrator for this section of the northeast. This network. Our work – here at the Academy, you understand – finished a week ago. Tomorrow, you would not have found any of us. But it is good that you have killed Blixa the Barghest. For that, we all thank you."

ACHIEVEMENT: *Manic Mansion.*

Now, to research Coreham College, turn to **287**.

To just go straight there, turn to **148**.

ACHIEVEMENTS CHECKLIST

As you find these ACHIEVEMENTS in play, check them off the list!

- ☐ $100K Penguin Suit Ruin
- ☐ A Million Lemmings
- ☐ Appetizer
- ☐ Be Seeing You
- ☐ But Thou Must
- ☐ Chaos Puppy
- ☐ Check Out the Big Brain on Six
- ☐ Come With Me if You Want to Live!
- ☐ Compulsive Hoarder
- ☐ Crème of the Crop
- ☐ Crushing Victory
- ☐ Dock Wolf
- ☐ Dying of Embarrassment
- ☐ Flying High
- ☐ Frugal
- ☐ Greed is Good
- ☐ I Wanna Be Your...
- ☐ I'm a Machine
- ☐ Landscaping
- ☐ Learning to Fly
- ☐ Lolly
- ☐ Low Profile
- ☐ Manic Mansion
- ☐ Me Go Far Away
- ☐ Mole Man
- ☐ My Best Me
- ☐ National Chaos
- ☐ One With Everything
- ☐ Phase One Went Smoo-oothly
- ☐ Secret Hunter One
- ☐ Secret Hunter Two
- ☐ Secret Hunter Three
- ☐ Secret Hunter Four
- ☐ Secret Hunter Five
- ☐ Secret Hunter Six
- ☐ Secret Hunter Seven
- ☐ Sir Robin
- ☐ Slanderous
- ☐ Sleeping With the Fishes
- ☐ Snatching Defeat From the Jaws of Victory
- ☐ Suspiciously Perfect
- ☐ Swooshy
- ☐ Terminally Indecisive
- ☐ That Went Well
- ☐ The Blinded Eye

- ☐ *The Bridgeburners*
- ☐ *The Final Hurdle*
- ☐ *The Headmaster*
- ☐ *The Replacements*
- ☐ *They Love Me In That Buffet*
- ☐ *Turncoat*
- ☐ *Twisty*
- ☐ *Virtue is its Own Reward*
- ☐ *You Had One Job*
- ☐ *You Have Been Naughty*

SUPER-ACHIEVEMENTS CHECKLIST

- ☐ Finish with a combined **MERC** + **MOUTH** + **FOCUS** of 20 or more: *Powerhouse.*

- ☐ Finish with {**CHAOS**} more than 15 and a combined **MERC** + **MOUTH** + **FOCUS** of 9 or less: *Hard Mode.*

- ☐ Finish with at least one star and a combined **MERC** + **MOUTH** + **FOCUS** of 2 or less: *Skin of Your Teeth.*

- ☐ Finish with {**DISCORD**} of 0: *Come Together.*

- ☐ Finish with {**DISCORD**} of 7 or more: *The Odd Couple.*

- ☐ Finish with {**PUZZLER**} of 6 or more: *Galaxy Brain.*

- ☐ Finish with {**SPORE-SEEDED**} of 1 or more: *Better Get That Looked At Sharpish.*

- ☐ Finish without cheating even once: *Iron Man.*

- ☐ Finish with a [**Sledgehammer**]: *Commit to the Bit.*

- ☐ Finish with a [**Sledgehammer**] and {**KUMQUATS**} of 1: *Seeing Things.*

- ☐ Finish with [**Adamantium Knuckles**], [**Crystal Monocle**], [**Diamond Smile**], [**Artisanal Stick Candy**] and [**FBI Badge**]: *Blinged Out.*

- [ ] Finish with any five useless items out of [Stethoscope], [Well Crank Handle], [Train Lever], [Crowbar], [Rusted Key], [Sparkling Powder]: *The Survival Horror Escape Kit*.

- [ ] Finish with any five unused consumable items out of [Tasty Energy Bar], [Carefully Unbranded High-Caffeine drink], [Tiger Amulet], [Timebomb], [Time Grenade], [Creepy Ball], [Caltrop], [Mutagenic Fluid], [Luckstone], [Pearl], [Candies]: *But I Might Need That Later*.

- [ ] Discover all 43 different items across multiple play-throughs: *Thorough, Impressive*.

- [ ] Discover all five endings: *The Completionist*.

- [ ] Discover all nine deaths: *Persistent*.

- [ ] Discover all seven Secret Hunter achievements: *Sherlock Holmes*.

- [ ] Collect all 17 super-achievements above this one: *Wunderbar!*

- [ ] Collect all 55 in-text achievements: *High Flyer*.

- [ ] Collect both High Flyer and Wunderbar!: *You are the GOAT*.

ABOUT THE AUTHOR

TIM DEDOPULOS is an unrepentant writer, editor, puzzle creator, game designer, and all-round word-slinger. He has written and/or edited just about everything it is possible to get paid to write and/or edit – books, manuals, games, puzzles, billboards, scripts, slogans, contracts, yadda yadda yadda – except plays. So far. He has used about a dozen pen-names which must remain absolutely secret. A long-time lover of science fiction, fantasy, horror, and comics, he is particularly interested in the places where prose, film and game are coming together. He can be found on Twitter as *@ghostwoods*, where he exclusively tweets absolute nonsense and insists on pretending the real world isn't happening.